COCKTALES

VOLUME THREE

A collection of eight erotic stories

Edited by Miranda Forbes

Published by Xcite Books Ltd – 2012
ISBN 9781908766441

Printed and bound by CPI Group (UK) Ltd, Croydon, CR0 4YY

Cover design by Sarah Davies

Contents

Deeds of Mercy
by Giselle Renarde

If Mercedes had to sum up her ridiculously complex sex life, it would go something like this: she used to date an older guy named Simon, who was all the while married to a woman called Florence. After years of hope and heartbreak, Mercedes broke it off with Simon and ultimately found herself engaged to a young guy named Anwar. Things were pretty solid until Mercedes met up with Simon again, purely by chance. She had no intention of hooking up with him ... until he made her an offer of cold, hard cash! With Mercedes' love of secrets, cocks, and infidelity, how could she refuse?

Mercedes' romantic world had grown into a man-eating monstrosity. She pictured it looking a lot like that giant plant from *Little Shop of Horrors*. She couldn't say why she kept seeing Simon. She really did love Anwar. It wasn't that she needed the money. Well, OK, the money was nice and it gave her a cheap thrill every time she added Sex-with-Simon cash to the Wedding-with-Anwar fund, but it's not like she was living at subsistence level. She didn't *need* it. But she liked it. She enjoyed the naughty thrill of prostituting herself to her married ex-lover while her husband-to-be remained oblivious.

Simon was very different as a paying customer than he'd been back when Mercedes was simply his doting mistress. He'd been so careful before. Now he took all sorts of chances. He didn't seem to give a fuck about getting caught. Maybe that was a product of now being able to say, 'What, this chick? I'm just paying her to suck my balls. Don't feel threatened, wifey.' Mercedes was sure the money made all the difference.

In the four years of their "couplehood", such as it was, Mercedes had never seen Simon's house. Never. She'd never seen his wife or his grown children, live in person or via any other medium. They'd been names, nothing more. In fact, his entire family was off-limits to her, though the rule itself remained unspoken.

That was then. Now, when Florence left town to visit her relatives for the weekend, Simon insisted Mercedes stay the night.

'At your house?' she asked.

'At my house,' he replied.

'But ...' Mercedes couldn't seem to locate the words required to express her trepidation. She wasn't even sure what precisely she was worried about. 'A whole night? That's ... a lot of hours. And we'll be ... sleeping together?'

Even over the phone, Simon sounded peeved. 'The whole time we were together, you begged me to spend the night with you. Now you don't want to?' He let out a *humph* and then said, 'I'll pay you per hour of sleep, if that's what you're so worried about.'

'No, no. I mean, yes, thank you, but ...' It finally clicked why she shouldn't be spending nights with her ex. 'Anwar! What am I supposed to tell Anwar?'

'Are you suddenly living together?' Simon asked in his rhetorical voice. 'No? Then what difference does it make where you sleep?'

Setting emotion aside, Mercedes looked at the situation from a business perspective: she could either spend

Saturday night falling asleep in front of Anwar's TV, or go to Simon's house, get fucked, get paid, go to sleep, get paid, and probably get fucked and paid once again come morning.

'Okay,' she said. 'You're right. I'll make it work.'

With a simple lie about a girls' night, Mercy set off to visit Simon's house for the first time. Her stomach tied itself in knots. She felt strange, knowing she'd be fucking some woman named Florence's husband in said woman named Florence's house. She felt sleazy about it. *Florence.* What an old lady name. Who was this woman named Florence? And why had Mercedes never wondered about her before now? Why did Simon cheat? Did this woman drive him to it? Was she horrible? Demeaning? Lame-o in bed? That must be it. Why else would Simon pay Mercedes for sex?

When she arrived at his door, Mercy expected Simon to grab her by the arm and swoop her inside, whispering, 'Did the neighbours see you?' Well, that isn't how it went down. Simon opened the door, casting a dark shadow across the stoop. He looked her up and down. Even as a dog-walking couple sauntered along the sidewalk, Simon smiled and told her she looked good enough to eat.

'I hope so,' she mumbled as she crept inside.

She thought she'd be curious about this house of Simon's, but her present feeling was exactly the opposite of curiosity. Mercedes tried not to look anywhere or see anything. Her senses dulled as he guided her by the arm. She stared down at her stocking feet against dark hardwood floors. Where were her shoes? She must have taken them off without realising.

There were pictures on the walls, but Mercedes wouldn't allow herself to look at them, not even to distinguish whether they were paintings of photographs.

Why had she come here? Business, pleasure, or pure masochism?

Soon, they came to be in a bedroom on the second floor of the house. When had they ascended a staircase? Mercy's mind was muddled with desire for absentia intermingled with desire for Simon. Despite her best efforts to find the man unattractive, she couldn't help being drawn to a body that defied age. Simon was always hard before his pants hit the ground, and his erections were thick and firm. When he fucked her, she always left satisfied. Better than satisfied, in fact ... Swollen and wet, sore and gasping for breath.

Now he seemed to be undressing her. No, scratch that. He seemed to have *undressed* her. Mercy's clothing hung over the back of a chair by the wooden desk. He was undressed too, but his clothes were on the floor. As always, his erection shot out in front of him like it was dowsing for wetness. Yes, Mercy realised, she was dripping for him. *Dripping.*

Simon's hard cock swung side to side as he strutted to the bedroom door and closed it. His body gleamed golden in the low light of two bedside lamps, which cast Mercy's shadow up against the adjacent wall. The room was stark, she noticed. But she didn't want to notice – anything – so she focused her attention on Simon. 'How do you want me?' she asked.

He could do anything to her. They'd agreed on a flat rate for any activity, except for the hours of sleep, which would cost extra. He usually started with a blowjob and finished off fucking her pussy. On rare occasions he fucked her ass, but he knew that hurt her and she really didn't like it all that much.

'I want to eat you,' he said. His forceful gaze burned like the glowing embers in the gas fireplace across from the bed. 'I miss the taste of your cunt. I want you on my tongue.'

That statement should have excited her, but Mercy was too entranced by the fireplace. It seemed brand new. Why would a couple with a lousy sex life get a gas fireplace installed in their bedroom? It wouldn't be for heat. There were plenty of other ways to heat up a bedroom. *God!* Simon and his wife couldn't possibly have a healthy sex life, could they? If they did, why did Simon have an affair with Mercedes? Why was he now paying her for the pleasure of eating her pussy? But what reason other than romance was there for a new fireplace in a bedroom?

Simon lifted her off her feet and dropped her on the bed. She bounced. The quilt was too pretty to mess up with her juices, but it was too late now. As Simon crawled up from the base of the bed, snarling like a wild thing, Mercy felt her inner thighs drench with juice. She crept back from him and drowned in a multitude of pillows. There was nowhere left to go. Only a wooden headboard remained at her back. Simon smiled in a sneering sort of way. 'Where are you going, Mercy? I thought you wanted me to eat you.'

'I do,' she said. Her heart fluttered as he grabbed her ankles and pulled her legs wide open.

'Nice work if you can get it,' he teased as he propelled his body between her legs like a trench soldier. 'You just sit back and enjoy my tongue on your pussy, and then you go home with your bra stuffed with cash. Wish I could find a job like that.'

His smugness would have pissed her off a few years ago. Now it turned her on. She couldn't bring herself to play the possession. 'It's too late for you,' she replied. 'Gotta be young and beautiful for a sweet position like this.'

'Sweet position?' Simon chuckled as he dove between her thighs. He went right at it and obviously didn't plan on letting up until she came hard enough to wake the neighbours. Back when they were a "couple", he'd been so dainty about eating her. He'd give her clit a few licks, she'd pretend he was God's gift, and then they'd move on to something else.

This was something else altogether. Simon was like a different person now that he was paying for sexual gratification. He tore into her like a beast. Holding her thighs wide apart, he pressed his face firm against her pussy so his lips met her clit and his nose planted in her trimmed bush. Mercy could feel the stubble on his chin against the base of her wet slit. His bristled cheeks scratched her outer lips like pleasant sadists as he took her clit in his hot mouth.

Mercy's whole body jumped. Simon sucked her clit like it was a tiny cock. This was something she'd never experienced before. Where had Simon picked up new material? Was it something his wife had taught him? No, couldn't be. Mercy was convinced they had next to no sex life. She'd convinced herself.

Sensation melted Mercy's mind. She bucked against Simon's face. Now she knew why guys got off on blowjobs. As Simon sucked her inner lips in with her clit, she tossed her head back and grabbed his with both hands. She thrust her hips at his face until she felt the scratch of his whiskers against her slit. His nose was flush to her bush. Could he even breathe down there? Mercy didn't give a fuck. She ran her pussy in tight circles against his muzzle. The prickle against her tender flesh generated an itch to fuck, and she hoped he'd get his cock inside her soon.

She'd have to come first, of course, but that was no

chore. The harder Simon sucked her clit, the harder it became to resist giving herself over to the looming wave of climax. She forced her clit into his mouth, nearly sitting upright as he splayed himself belly-down on the bed. With his head in her hands, she pushed his face against her pussy the way porn star men do to porn star women when they're getting their blowjobs. She felt almost guilty to treat him this way, especially when he'd be paying her in the morning, but she was so close to coming she couldn't stop now.

Finally, the urge to move was subsumed by the urge to receive pleasure. Mercy held Simon's face against her pussy and screamed as he sucked her like mad.

When she finished screaming and could take no more pleasure or pain, Mercy closed up her legs and fell back into the cluster of pillows. Either her eyes were closed or she'd just gone blind. Her orgasm had so overtaken her she couldn't figure out which was the case. She finally realised her eyes were indeed closed, and she decided to open them. When she did, she saw two things: Simon looming between her knees with his long cock looking like it wanted to get up inside her, and, on the mantle behind him, a wedding photo. She must only have spent a few seconds looking at it, but she recognised a youthful Simon as the groom. The woman in the white gown was obviously his bride.

Mercy was shocked by this photo. Not because it was a wedding photo – she obviously knew Simon was married. This photo told her one thing she'd never known about the man: his wife was pug fugly. Worse than pug fugly! She had a face like a bulldog after a bar brawl. And in her wedding photo! A woman always looked her best on her wedding day. If Florence looked like that when she was married, imagine what she must look like now!

'I want to fuck you,' Simon growled. Slipping off the bed, he flipped her from her back to her front. 'I want it doggy style.'

'Yeah.' She felt too distracted to sound sexy. Then her gaze fell to another photo. This one sat on the night table right beside Mercy's face. It was definitely Florence – the face was an older, more wrinkled, an even uglier version of the one on the mantle. She looked like a Halloween hag. Could this really be Simon's wife? Christ, no wonder he was willing to pay Mercedes for sex!

As Mercy lay staring at the figure in the photo, Simon climbed on the bed and splayed her legs as far apart as they would go. That action jolted her into the moment. Her pussy clenched in anticipation. She closed her eyes, but the image of Simon's ugly wife seemed burnt into her retinas.

When Simon grabbed her hips, Mercy raised her ass to him. He knew exactly what he wanted these days, and he lifted her up to the perfect height. After piling up pillows under her pelvis, he wasted no time going at her. He rammed her so hard it panged inside, but Mercy didn't care. The pang of a gleaming purple cockhead against her insides hurt less than the sting of resentment in knowing what Simon had stayed with throughout their years together.

He scratched her back with sharp little nails as he fucked her pussy. The pain felt wonderful. He smacked her ass cheeks until they turned red. That felt even better. But why had Simon stayed with such an ugly woman when he could have had Mercedes? As his cock raced in and out of her hot, wet pussy, Mercy realised how ridiculously narcissistic she was being. Maybe Florence was the nicest, sweetest, most internally beautiful person in the world! Maybe Simon had a thousand reasons to

8

stay married to her.

Grunting like a troll, Simon threw his sweating chest on top of Mercy's back. The pillows piled underneath her pelvis held their butts aloft, but Simon grasped her wrists and held them down as he fucked her. She felt trapped in his body now, as her mind was trapped in a cycle of, 'Why her and not me? Why choose ugly when he could have beautiful? What's so great about Florence?'

Even as Simon grabbed Mercy's breasts and groaned, the pleasure of fucking couldn't dispel the multitude of questions. Simon propelled his hips at Mercy's ass and bit down hard on her shoulder. Mercy screeched. Pain soared through her body. Her blood sizzled in her veins. She was sweating all over this pretty marriage quilt, and her pussy juice now graced a stack of throw pillows. As her cunt clamped down on Simon's orgasmic cock, a series of words tumbled out of her mouth unhindered: 'My God, Simon, your wife is one pug ugly motherfucker!'

The room went silent as Simon rolled off Mercy's back. The bed bounced beneath them. Was there any utterance crueller than the one that had just passed through her lips? She'd insulted Simon's wife! This was the woman he'd been married to for how many years? And Mercy called her ugly. Why would she say that? Was she jealous? Even with her engagement to Anwar, was she still subconsciously coveting Simon? Was she still in love with him? Or was this wife of his simply unconscionably ugly?

'God, I know she is,' he finally said. 'And she always was. It's embarrassing, isn't it?'

With a growl, Simon pulled Mercedes down from her Princess-and-the-Pea stack of pillows. Tossing her onto her back, he rolled on top. His spent cock drooled forgotten spurts of come against her leg as he took her breast in his mouth and sucked. Everything he did to her was animalistic now. There was an intangible sort of brutality in his every move.

After a moment of vicious nipple sucking, Mercedes asked, 'Why did you marry her?'

Simon pressed Mercedes' breasts together. When he spoke, his voice resonated from somewhere inside her cleavage. 'Back in the day, she used to be great in the sack.' He laughed, and collapsed beside her on the bed. Grabbing a pillow for his head, he squeezed her in close to his body and closed his eyes. 'Same reason I stick with you.'

Mercy's heart froze in her chest. When Simon pressed a cruel kiss against her temple, she tried to ease herself away, but he only wrapped her tighter in his arms. The implications were too many, and too jarring. Her mind raced. Sure, he was paying her to stay the night, but Mercedes didn't sleep a wink.

Tropical Paradise
by Velvet Tripp

Ellie had worked there for over three years, and she loved her life at the zoo. She'd always wanted to work with animals. The thought of a nine-to-five office job left her cold. Here in the tropical house, she didn't work office hours and she certainly wasn't cold.

At this time of day, all the visitors had gone, and she was expected to hose down the walkways, remove any litter and check the birds and the temperature as she moved around. Despite all the computer-controlled heaters and sprays, a manual check was the only way to ensure the overnight safety of the house inhabitants. And since she'd met Sam, whose usual job was taking care of the big cats, it had become a very pleasant task indeed to be the last on duty.

Tall blond men were Ellie's thing, and she'd spotted Sam on her first day. It was a couple of months before they'd actually been introduced. He was slightly older than her at 29, and a more experienced keeper. He was lucky. He had classic good looks, a great smile and a way with animals that made him a favourite with women. Ellie couldn't believe her luck when he'd asked her out.

He was due any moment. Her heart was already racing. Their sex life had been eventful, to say the least. Both got off on a bit of danger and they'd decided on this – their latest adventure – after talking about just how hot and steamy the tropical house got once the doors were closed to the public. The boss would never know. He was off to Africa the following morning to oversee the importation of a rare and endangered species of snake, and had left early to prepare.

As she walked around, checking her charges carefully, she mused on their relationship so far. It had begun as a torrid affair. The kind of mutual attraction that can be dangerous, that can fool you into thinking that passion was love. Then, as she'd found in the past, you could come down to Earth with a big bump when it all fell apart. Ellie knew that for her this was actually turning to love, and for a while she'd waited for the big let-down. But it never came. Sam had, to her delight and relief, returned her affections and they had formed a strong bond. Spending more and more time together came naturally and easily. Their interests overlapped in so many areas that others had begun to see them as the perfect couple. Ellie found that their bond only enhanced their sex life. She didn't feel the need to hold anything back, and neither, it seemed, did Sam.

A loud call caught her attention, and she looked up into the canopy above her. Ellie watched as one of the birds of paradise displayed his magnificent iridescent feathers, intent on catching the interest of a female. He shimmered his resplendent tail, stretching his neck to show off the gorgeous plumage on his chest and calling for all he was worth. He was a handsome bird, tireless in his efforts to secure a mate. As she watched, the female approached him and he began his full courtship dance.

Sam appeared, freshly showered and minus his shirt, behind the huge palm tree overlooking the slate path. He cut a fine figure, his hairless chest rippling with muscle, built by the demands of the job. Ellie thought he was just as gorgeous as the bird she'd just been watching, the one now mating above them. Sam's hair flopped down over his eyes as he strolled towards her, grinning. Ellie was looking forward to this. Under her zoo uniform she had only stockings, bra and panties. After all, she *was* working in a hot environment, she would have explained if anyone had noticed her changing that lunchtime. Just the fact that she'd done that had kept her anticipation level high.

Sam dropped his work bag on a bench and sat down, beckoning Ellie to join him. Moments later they were locked in a fervent embrace. Sam nuzzled Ellie's neck and gently nibbled her ear while stroking her thigh. Goosebumps ran down her spine. He still had that magical way of making her feel like the sexiest woman on the planet. She returned his enthusiasm, running her hand down his naked chest, past his belt and down to his groin. He was evidently as excited as she, judging by the huge bulge she found there.

The atmosphere in the tropical house was, as they'd fantasised, hot and steamy even before they started. Perfume from the sweetest flowers wafted through the air. Tropical birds perched high above them called out. Condensation from all that steam dripped from the huge banana and palm leaves around them. Rainbow-coloured butterflies alighted on them as they embraced. Without the cost of a long trip to paradise, they had it here for free. For Ellie this was pure decadence.

Sam began to unfasten Ellie's work top, a huge smile on his face when he realised just what she hadn't worn for work that afternoon. Slipping his fingers inside her bra, he massaged her nipple into life, leaving her breathing heavily. Now she grinned. Kneeling in front of him, she spent few moments removing the belt and undoing his jeans. His cock was no longer contained, and sprung to its full length in front of her. She began slowly, licking and teasing the tip, running her tongue around the glans. Sam exhaled loudly, his pleasure obvious. She teased a little more, running her fingers gently up the shaft and down again. Then she licked her way from the tip to the base, cupping his balls in her hands, squeezing lightly. He groaned, eyes now closed and hands resting on Ellie's shoulders, urging her to continue. She wrapped her tongue around the tip, gradually allowing more of his cock in her mouth until she had it all. Sucking and licking, moving up and down his full length, she felt him swell even more, bulging with desire.

He grabbed her hair, pulling gently. 'Not yet,' he sighed. 'I've got plans for you.'

Ellie pulled back and looked up at Sam, who was grinning wildly. She loved his self-control. He could put off his own climax indefinitely and they usually made the very most of that. Tonight would be no exception.

'Come here,' he said.

Ellie stood up before her lover. He slowly removed her work trousers, tracing his fingers over her inner thighs as he did so, and leaning forward to kiss her flat, toned stomach. Ellie drew in a sharp breath. This was going to be good, if not great. 'Come on,' he said, taking her by the hand and leading her through the palms and bananas to a clearing normally used by staff to access the bird cages. There, already arranged, was a picnic blanket and a bottle of wine with glasses. 'I dropped these in while you were doing your checks. Sneaky, eh?'

Ellie was delighted. 'Sneaky but commendable. No one can see us, even through the glass, from here.'

'Exactly.' He poured two glasses of wine and handed one to Ellie.

They both burst out laughing. 'This is fun,' Ellie giggled finally. 'At work but at play. At home but in the jungle. Never mind *Sex in the City*. This beats it hands down and we haven't even really started!'

They sipped the wine slowly, wanting to savour the experience. 'You know, I've had this dream since I was little,' Ellie told him. 'About being in a jungle, feeling so wild and free, running around in little more than a loin cloth. It must have been the old Tarzan film that set me off.'

'Well, I don't know about loin cloths. No clothes is even better,' Sam replied. 'And you're not little any more. Shall we do the grown-up version?'

Ellie just grinned and raised her glass. 'I'll drink to that!' she said, draining the rest of her wine.

With that he took her glass, placed it down out of the way and pushed her onto her back. He leant over her, kissing her eyelids each in turn, then kissed her on the mouth. She responded eagerly, kissing back with passion and tongue. He nuzzled her neck, reaching out and running his hands over her breasts, still enclosed in her sexy black bra. A quick, practised flick of his fingers on her back soon removed the obstacle. Her pert, sensitive breasts now exposed, he began circling the nipples with his tongue. She gasped. He began to massage one with his fingers, rolling it around until it was as hard as a little pebble. Then the other one. By now Ellie's skin was as damp as her pussy. Taking a nipple into his mouth, he sucked, licked and nibbled until Ellie was writhing with pleasure. He'd learnt very early on just how sensitive her nipples were, and loved to see her squirm.

His hands ran down over her breasts and stomach, stopping short at her pubic bone. He liked to keep her on the edge, and she would not complain. She loved him to take his time, take her slowly to the edge and back again before the climax. When she finally got there, she knew it would be more intense, more mindblowing.

'I have a little treat for you,' he said unexpectedly, and pulled out from his bag a silk blindfold. This was new, but Ellie found herself tingling with excitement as he slipped it over her eyes. 'Now you have to concentrate on what you can feel. There's nothing like not being able to see to concentrate the mind on your other senses.'

She grinned. Boy, he was good. Always new surprises.

He was right too. As Ellie lay there, she inhaled the sweet, damp earth mixed with the heady scent of gardenias growing nearby. Every sound seemed more distinct. The birds were still calling above them, still mating as she listened. Her skin cried out for his touch. She would not be disappointed. Now he knelt astride her, and he had more in store. Ellie felt something extremely gentle and soft flicking over her skin. The touch was light, like butterflies' wings flitting over her skin, and wherever he touched, messages of desire flew to her pussy and brain. Her skin, now super-sensitive, tingled with every sensation. He traced over her breasts, alighting gently on her nipples, caressing them until the tension became almost unbearable.

He moved down her stomach, over her pubis, between her thighs. She spread her legs in an unconscious response to his attentions. His hands moved to push her knees together – a move that surprised her until she felt the soft material of her panties sliding down her thighs, over her knees and ankles and almost magically disappearing. By now she was so responsive to every touch, she could even feel his breath over her skin as he stripped her, and shuddered with delight. She lifted her arse to help him, eager for the barrier to be out of the way, anticipation building in her mind and pussy, which was already wet.

Sam was going to savour this. He sat back on his heels and looked at Ellie, now naked, blindfold and sprawled on the floor in front of him amid the vivid exotic flowers planted below huge palm trees draped with exotic vines. She looked so beautiful, he sometimes couldn't believe his luck. Her small frame made her look so delicate, yet she could be very strong and determined. As they'd grown closer, he'd also found out what an animal she could be in bed. Her pert, neat breasts topped with small, dark and extremely hard nipples begged for his attention. Ellie gasped in surprise and delight as he leant forward and took one into his mouth. He flicked the other breast with the exotic bird feathers he'd collected and bound into a fan shape especially for this.

Then slowly he kissed, flicked and nibbled his way over his lover's naked body until she shivered with excitement, stretching out like one of Sam's panthers. Kneeling between her parted thighs, he brushed the feathers over her thighs, and lightly over her parted, damp labia. Ellie quivered beneath the touch, her swelling clit now pushing them open further. Sam couldn't resist any longer. Keeping the fan in his hand, he moved his face towards the object of his desire.

First he blew on her clit gently, eliciting yet another gasp. He loved her natural perfume, and inhaled it with anticipation pulsing through his veins as he began running his tongue around her labia. Circling slowly and deliberately around her clit, he reached out with the fan and dusted it over her breasts and down her abdomen. As he did so he flicked his tongue over her swollen button. By now Ellie was squirming, her breath shallow and fast. He repeated the motion over and over, until her hips were rising to meet his mouth, and finally she cried out 'Please!

Now. Give it to me now.' The magic words. He crawled up between her legs. They were both sweating in the sultry atmosphere and the heat of the experience, and he slithered over her eager body, until his cock was nudging her welcoming vagina.

She rose to meet him, pushing herself onto his eager, pulsing cock. As he inched inside her, she felt his size filling her, stretching her, and still she strained for more. She liked it deep, and Sam knew it. He grinned as he lifted her buttocks, positioning himself to slam hard into her as she reached fever pitch. They moved in perfect synchrony, matching each other's passion thrust for thrust, Sam watching his lover's lips part and cry as she reached her zenith. He loved to watch her come. Her fingers dug into his back as she writhed with wave after wave of sheer rapture. He waited, gently moving inside her now, allowing her to revel in the final moments of her orgasm. Ellie relaxed a little, sighing with a huge smile. He removed the blindfold, just so he could see the look in her eyes. Kissing her passionately, he began to build up the strokes again. He knew she would want more, and she was going to get it.

'Hang on,' Ellie gasped. 'Let me turn over.' Sam grinned. His favourite position! Tenderly he withdrew, and in a moment Ellie was kneeling, doggie-style in front of him. She wanted it deep! He knelt behind her, her pussy dripping invitingly in front of him. Her arse, pert and firm, wiggled teasingly. He again pushed his pounding cock into her, slowly making his way as deep as he could inside her. She began to rock backwards towards him, and they were soon matching each other's strokes. Their fervour increased the pace little by little until they were pounding together at a frantic pace. Sam slapped her arse and Ellie cried and moaned, her arms stretched out, grasping at the air, sweat dripping from her as she came for the second time. Sam allowed himself to let go, and Ellie's orgasm was prolonged as she felt his waves of pleasure pulsing deep inside her.

It was much later when they reached Ellie's flat, and later still that they finally crawled into bed, freshly showered. 'Good job we're off tomorrow,' Ellie said, yawning. 'It's 6.30 a.m.' Sam looked exhausted but very contented.

'Yeah, we can spend tomorrow planning for the real thing,' he replied.

'Real thing? What are you talking about?'

'I've saved the best until last. A surprise for you. Remember when we applied to the boss to do a field trip? There wasn't any funding then to do it, but he reckons our dedication has earned us some more experience in the field, and there's new research starting in South America. The boss caught me just as he was leaving his office. We've got the gig!'

Ellie squealed with delight. This was the chance they'd waited two years for. A real tropical paradise they'd spend three whole months in. Quite apart from the career-furthering opportunities it would give them, they'd be able to spend three whole months in their dream environment.

'When do we go?'

'Not until the end of the season here. We'll be away over Christmas, come back sometime late January.'

'Fantastic,' she said. 'Where are we staying?'

'Well, from what I understand the safest place in a jungle national park is a treehouse. Fancy that? Up in the canopy, just imagine the scents and sights. The treehouse swaying to our rhythm. Even better than the tropical house. The real thing.'

'Mmm,' was her reply. Ellie fell asleep wrapped in Sam's arms. He was sure he could hear her purring contentedly. She could picture herself, lying on a bed of cool palm leaves and flower petals, wet through in the steamy atmosphere with the song of tropical birds, the vision of rainbow-coloured butterflies and the thought of her lover's cock slipping inside her resounding in her brain, safely swaying in their treehouse.

Much better than Tarzan any day of the week.

Exemplary Employee
by Charlotte Stein

He always comes to my house wearing a sort of tunic, pristine and white and pinned at one shoulder. Like a doctor, from the future. His trousers usually match, too, and so do his little white shoes.

He should look prim or weird, I know, but he never does. He looks like a professional, with his fine blond hair brushed down smooth and flat. And his little case, filled with professional things like oils and lotions and exfoliating mitts.

They are the kind of things that any masseuse would wear, or carry around. And he has the kind of accent best suited to masseuses – an accent you expect. Sort of Swedish or maybe Norwegian, with few correct English words in between it all.

I think he's memorised the right phrases to say, when he visits a client. *Would you like to lie down now*, that sort of thing. *Shall I put on the music? Do you want the jasmine? Soft, or hard?*

Though he usually doesn't ask now. He knows what I like, and what I don't like. He's very good – very business-like and utterly thorough. All of his clients speak very highly of him, and I can see why. Who wouldn't want a tall, blond, handsome Swedish man coming to rub his hands over their bare bodies, twice a week?

It used to be once, but I've upped it since then. Now

that I know that he's so well trained, and careful, and diligent. I mean – just look at that pristine white. He is obviously excellent at his job. His natural manner seems to be one of utter calm and steadiness, which is a perfect match, really, for this kind of work.

'Would you like to remove your clothes?' he says, and I do. I used to pop into the bathroom and come out in a towel, when he first started coming. But now I don't see the need, I really don't. He obviously divorces himself very successfully from his work – why, I might as well be getting a massage from a robot.

A tall, handsome robot, who last week said to me: 'No, no girlfriend', when I asked him if he had one. So I had said: 'Boyfriend, then?' But he had simply laughed, and replied, 'Girls. I like girls.' And then, after a moment, the strangest thing: 'You have excellent buttocks, Miss Hartford.'

Which is something I'd never really thought about, before. I suppose it might be because he generally massages a lot of older ladies, and perhaps my bottom seems a bit firmer in comparison. Though then again my breasts aren't quite as perky as they could be, but he still tells me that they're excellent too.

So maybe he just says it to everyone, to make them feel better.

'Can I massage the breasts?' he asks, which seems odd. Because usually, he doesn't ask at all. I mean, it's part of an all-over-body massage, isn't it? What would be the point, if he missed out a large area on my chest?

'Of course,' I tell him, and he slides oil-slick fingers over my nipples, in firm decisive strokes.

I must confess, I get a little tingle, when he does it. I've had them before, of course, because he's very good at his job and sometimes the whole thing leaves me quite breathless. But this seems like a little bit more than in previous sessions, and it could be because every time he squeezes my breasts in his large hands, he finishes on a slight tug of my nipples – which are erect by this point, naturally.

'Very good,' he says, and I wonder what he means. It's hard to tell, because he has such an impassive face. Such serene blue eyes – and oh, that delightful little cleft in his chin. Though if he were ugly, I'm sure the whole thing would be just as nice. It's lovely to have a bit of human contact, you know.

'Turn over now,' he says, which is a little disappointing. It was making me feel quite flushed, all that massaging of my breasts. If it had gone on a little longer, I don't think I would have complained.

'Shhh,' he says. 'Don't worry, don't worry.'

Though I can't say why. Do I seem worried? I'm not in the least bit concerned, in his capable, professional hands.

Though when I glance to the left, I notice he's unbuttoned that strange clasp, which holds his uniform closed at his left shoulder. I mean, it's not gaping open, or anything. And I can't really say much – perhaps it just came undone on its own, or maybe he was feeling a little hot. But still ... it's odd.

And it's odd when he says *mmmm* too, as his hands glide up and down my back. Odd and entirely pleasant – he *really* knows what he's doing.

I squirm, when I feel him drizzle more oil all over me. Now I'm practically sopping, when he starts rubbing me again. So it's not really a surprise, when his hand accidentally slides right over the hills of my buttocks, and all the way in between.

I don't say anything, however. He's such a

professional that he's probably mortified, to find that his slippery fingers are between the cheeks of my bottom. Either that, or this is just a new part of the massage – which I think it could well be. I mean, what's an all-over-body massage, if it avoids a great big giant place like ... there?

He clearly knows what he's doing.

'You like me to stop?' he asks – see what I mean about his politeness? Just so charming.

'Of course not,' I reply. 'You do what you think is best, Sven.'

I don't think his real name is Sven. But I've never said anything, and see no reason to mention it now.

'Very good,' he says, and he sounds a bit breathless, poor thing. It must be the heat in here – it's positively scorching.

So I tell him to take some of his uniform off. You know, just to alleviate matters. But oh dear me, he goes for the top half first and I can't think what to say to that, apart from the little chuckle that comes out of me. Oh dear me no, he can't take the top off – that's the part of his uniform that marks him out as a diligent professional.

No, it has to be the trousers. Just the trousers, and maybe the shoes too.

Now he's just in his underpants and his white tunic, sliding his hand back and forth between my legs. He gently parts them so that he can work freely and easily, and tells me that he's going to use a soothing, scent-free oil for the best results.

Though in all honesty, I can't see why he needs it there. I seem to be quite well lubricated already, and one of his long, thick fingers slides into my sex no problems at all. He's breathing fairly hard and high now, which I suppose is to be expected. I mean, it must be hard work to

24

have to reach a little way under someone's body, like this, in order to get at their clit. And he has his thumb in my pussy while he goes about it, so I can't imagine it's easy.

'You like?' he asks. 'You like?'

And at the very least, he deserves a yes. Even when he slides one finger of his free hand between my buttocks, again, and passes it over my arsehole – he still deserves a yes. After all, it's not unpleasant. Not even when he pushes it in a little way, and fingers me there while he strokes my pussy.

'So good,' he moans, because I am, you know. I'm a very good client, indeed. I give myself over to all these soaring, jostling tingles the minute he tells me I should, though whether he intended to order me to *come now, come now*, I'm not entirely sure.

His English just isn't very good at all.

When he comes again the next day – I asked him for an extra appointment, and considering my generous tip he was only too happy to oblige – we get right down to business. But this time, I ask him if I might lie on my back. I explain that I thoroughly enjoyed the breast massage, and a little ghost of a smile plays on his pale lips.

There's nothing wrong with taking pride in your work, I want to tell him, but instead I just strip out of my clothes and lie down on the bed.

He gets straight to work – of course he does. Slicking his hands with oil, drizzling it over my tight nipples and my freshly waxed mound. He's an artist, really.

'You feel nice and relaxed now?' he asks, and I give him what he clearly wants. I tell him that he did an excellent job yesterday, and that I was thrilled with the results.

At which he smiles again, and begins easing all that oil over my waiting body. Slow strokes, at first, but then longer. And longer. From the hollow of my throat, to the jut of my hips and down, all the way down. I must say I'm quite ticklish, in the foot area, so when he gets there, of course I laugh.

His expression is quite startled and odd, when the little sound escapes from me. Almost hurt, I think, and then it occurs to me – why, he just wants to be sure he's doing a good job. What sort of person likes having someone laugh at them, while they're in the middle of such a delicate operation?

So I explain – I'm just ticklish, there. At which he relaxes once more. He relaxes so much that he takes his trousers off again, and it doesn't escape my notice that he's wearing different underpants. These ones are quite small and almost transparent – what Americans might call tighty-whities, I suppose – and they reveal a lot.

It makes me want to avert my eyes, but when you really think about it, that would be impossibly rude. There he is, complimenting my body and rubbing oil all over me, and I'm not showing the slightest bit of appreciation for his.

So I stare, at the distinct shape of his erect cock, through the thin material.

Of course I'm not the least bit offended. By it being erect, I mean. I suppose other women might be, but I find it as flattering as I'm sure he intends it. Plus I have to feel some measure of sympathy for the poor fellow. He clearly has a large appendage. It must be terribly difficult to hide any arousal, while massaging supple young bodies.

And especially when he has his hands between my legs again, and is rubbing my slit gently, up and down, up and down.

26

'Yes, very nice,' he says, and I feel so obliged to tell him the same. Thankfully, however – being the well-trained masseuse that he is – he does it for me.

'You like this,' he says, and touches the angular shape in his underwear. 'You like it, good. Watch it while I massage.'

I wonder if he intends it as some sort of meditation or concentration technique. You know – focusing on one single point in order to drain out the body's impurities, and the like. And he's right, because I can feel my body's impurities draining out of me right now. He has two fingers in my pussy and he's rubbing my clit with the heel of his palm and I'm shivering all over, like a mad thing.

'That's it,' he says. 'Let it go, let it all go.'

And I tingle just like I did yesterday – at his behest, with his large, strong hands between my legs.

However, this time is different. This time, he does not begin to pack up, once his hands are off me, and away. Instead, he continues to kneel by my liquid body, breathing hard. He tells me over and over, *very good*, and then finally, after a while, says something he's never said before.

Though I suppose all of these are new techniques and explorations, so it seems rather pointless to halt proceedings now.

'Oh, I am very stressful,' he says, poor chap. Then, almost haltingly and with his eyes sort of sliding away from me: 'Would you help me with the stressfulness?'

And I think to myself: well. What sort of decent-minded Christian woman would refuse? Hasn't he been utterly considerate and attentive to my needs? Professional in all respects? Of course he has.

I would only be too happy to relieve any stress he has, and I tell him so immediately.

He smiles – almost bashfully, I think – shortly before I ask him if he'd like to take his tunic off. I mean, I'd prefer for him to keep it on. But if the tension is all in his shoulders, then I'll have to work there.

But he shakes his head, and explains further for me, patiently. I'm so glad he's patient, because of course I have no experience with this sort of thing. He is the masseuse, and he's going to have to guide me if he wants a successful relieving of his stress.

'No, no. It is in this area,' he says, and points to his groin.

Oh, what a dafty I am! I should have *known*. Clearly he is in dire need of stress relief, in that particular area. As my husband would have said, were he still about: *good one, Margot! Gone and cocked it, yet again!*

Which I suppose is a rather appropriate term, given the circumstances. *Cocked it*.

Sven tugs those little underpants down, and I sit up, ready to set to work. I crack my knuckles – you know, just to get everything nice and limber – and then await instructions. I'm sure he's going to give me instructions – and the more detailed the better, obviously.

I mean, what sort of person could perform such a delicate massage, without some sort of help?

'Just grab it,' he says, so I do. It's as big as I suspected and curving right up to his stomach, so it's not a hard task to accomplish. Although I do run into some trouble almost immediately – my hands are slippery with massage oil without me really intending them to be, and he ... well. He's all messy and leaking, so it's hard to get a good grip. My hand slides and slithers along the length of his shaft, and he makes the most impressive sound.

Like the one I made, not so long ago. Like someone letting go and all that sort of thing.

'Yes,' he says. 'Yes, yes – good girl, oh good girl.'

Which is very nice of him. I don't think I'm doing this very well – my husband was never really one for it, you understand – but he makes sure I know he appreciates it. He even thrusts back and forth into the unsteady but tight circle of my fist, to facilitate matters.

And when that isn't enough, he graciously offers advice.

'Both hands,' he blurts out. 'Use both hands.'

So I do. I get one hand right at the root, and one close and sometimes sliding over the very red tip, and I massage and rub and squeeze. And I suppose I must be doing something right, because his head goes right back and he groans as loud as anything. He *whines* too, which I've never heard before – a very Swedish sounding whine, if there is such a thing, with lots of gasping in between.

'Harder,' he gasps. 'Rub it harder – ah, yes!'

I'm really putting my back into it now. He shows me with his own hands how to twist one this way, while I twist one the other – which sounds really painful, but it makes him say lots of the word *yes*, and the slit at the tip of his prick lets out a little drop of liquid. So I guess he must enjoy it.

Plus it's a real massage, then, isn't it? All this deep twisting and turning, getting all of him in my two small hands. It must be how the real professionals do it, I suppose.

I wonder if the real professionals shake all over, when they do it. And I wonder if their clients shout out, desperately: 'Oh – I'm coming, I'm coming!'

Or maybe that's just him and me.

And he does, you know. He does it all over my thighs, because I've shuffled up very close to him and I'm kneeling like this – so it's very easy for his spend to get all over me. There's a lot of it too, and when he sees what a frightful mess he's made, he seems very embarrassed.

But I tell him not to worry. He can easily clean me up – why, there must be a hundred ways he could go about it! Like lying down on top of me so it all mingles into our skin, sticky and slick at first, but soon rubbed down to nothing.

All over body to body massage, he calls this. I try to tell him that our half-hour is up, but he won't have any of it. 'No,' he says. 'We have to do this.'

So I lie there, while he rubs that rough tunic over my still stiff nipples, and his great bare thighs between my spread legs. He squirms slickly where we're naked, and coarsely where we're not, and sometimes, oh, his body catches mine, just right.

I can feel that thigh, right up against my clit. It's a *very* good massage, this way. So good that we go on for quite a while and I think I might, you know, go over – I'm certainly making quite a bit of noise, which he seems to appreciate.

But then I notice that he appears to be erect again, against my belly. At which point he tells me that he's going to change the massage, slightly. To make it more comfortable for both of us.

I tell him that it's quite comfortable enough for me, but he says no, no, and he looks so pleasant and handsome above me – those pale eyes, suddenly flashing – and he's such a professional, that why should I say no?

And of course, he's right. His prick fits very snugly along the seam of my sex, rubbing through all the slickness I'm sure I should be embarrassed about. I even turn my head to one side, but he says *oh no, no. Don't look away – so pretty*.

He's a good sort. He rubs that big thick head of his

cock right over my clit, over and over. Fast, and then slow, and then fast again, and all the while he describes to me how smooth everything is, and wet, and good. He tells me that I'm very good to him, and I think it's those words that make me tingle all over in that breathless, twisting sort of way.

I call out the name which is probably not his, and my clit swells against the press of his cock, and he says *Margot* but pronounces it *Mar-got*, which seems very odd because I thought Margot was a Swedish name.

Though I hardly care if he's got it right or not, because his face is all twisted up and he's panting very hard, again, and I think this all-over-body massage thing is very good indeed, because it wasn't long since he relieved a bit of stress the last time, and he's already going for another.

My husband couldn't go for another after a week, never mind 20 minutes. But then I always said about Sven – he's very skilled. And he must know that sperm is good for the skin, because he's doing it all over me again, right between my legs, all over my clit and my pussy.

I feel it long after he's collapsed on top of me, trickling between the cheeks of my bottom. Or maybe that's just me, because I don't think I've ever had two of those tingles in such a short space of time either.

It's really a testament to his thoroughness. I mean, if there were a performance review to fill out, I know exactly what I'd say. Exemplary employee, really – top marks. Very thorough and professional, always on time and never over stepping his mark.

Not to mention absolutely excellent at making me come.

Retail Seduction
by Tabitha Rayne

Selena traces the soft fabric over her arm. It feels so luscious and rich she puts it to her cheek then looks around furtively before winding it around her hands and wrists lifting it closer to her neck.

'Can I help you?' The assistant appears from nowhere making Selena jump.

'Oh, erm, yes, where are the fitting rooms please?' The assistant looks quizzically at the black velvet scarf which is the only item in Selena's arms.

'It's over there by the lingerie at the back of the shop. You might want to take some other garments in as well, madam?'

Selena nods quickly and grabs the nearest shirt. She makes her way to the changing rooms and tugs at the scarf, which has wound its way tighter around her wrist constricting her hand. It feels good and she takes the tag offered by the changing room assistant.

'Just the two items?' Selena nods again, afraid to speak in case her voice has the tell tale quiver that would alert her and everyone else to her arousal. It always takes her by surprise; it can come from nowhere, but when it does, her need is so great, so overwhelming, that she has to find a place to go, and fast. She scurries to the furthest cubicle and pulls across the heavy curtain. Damn it, she thinks, the only changing rooms in town without a lock …

'My name's Debbie, let me know if you need anything.' Selena clutches the shirt and scarf to her chest, but is relieved when the assistant wanders off without peeking in. Selena waits, ears pricked, to hear the clack of Debbie's heels retreating back in to the main shop. Paranoia overtakes her and she takes one last peek around the curtain. Nothing. All the other cubicles are empty with the curtains flung back. Satisfied that she is alone, Selena examines herself in the mirror. She looks nervous, frail. It annoys her and she refocuses to the thick black coils snaking their way around her wrist. Her hand is beginning to tingle with the constriction and she carefully unwraps it, feeling the blood rush back in, warm and engorging.

She exhales deeply and fully and looks at herself in the mirror again. That's better. Her posture is now erect but relaxed and her head is tipped back slightly so she is looking down at herself. She breathes in and fills her lungs, her chest, her breasts. She loves watching her own body as it begins its erotic arousal. Her lips are full and red and she watches her tongue glide over them moistening them. She takes the scarf again and pulls it tight between her hands and snaps it taut. As she watches her reflection she imagines she is watching herself through Jim's eyes. She slowly lifts the velvet strap up past her chest, pausing to drag it across her nipples. She smiles as they spring to attention yearning for her to touch them again but she resists and slowly continues the journey to her neck. She lifts her head high and tips it back further tilting it from side to side to examine her slender neck. She rubs the fabric back and forward over her throat, teasing herself. She feels heat between her legs and watches her feet as they move apart, her heels gliding easily over the lino flooring. She has a skirt on; it is longer than she usually wears as she had treated herself wearing suspenders and stockings that morning. She pushes her back into the wall and slides down it slightly to try and ruffle her skirt higher. She manages to get it a couple of inches, but not enough to see the thick black band at the top of her nylons. It frustrates her, but this is part of the game to herself. She can't make it too easy.

She drags her attention back to the scarf and pulls it tighter around her throat, pressing her fists into the cubicle wall. She watches as her cheeks redden and she gasps as excitement floods between her legs. She winds the scarf tighter around her fists and tries, once again, to hitch up her skirt. For every inch it rides up she has to split her legs slightly further apart to keep it there. It's a good pay off. She is practically squatting by the time she catches a glimpse of her suspenders. She opens her knees to reveal her dampening knickers. She wishes she hadn't put them on. Her breathing is becoming a shallow pant and sweat is forming on her forehead and down her back. She squeezes her pussy tight and almost squeals out with the pleasure it gives her to be so hot and turned on by herself.

She reaches the strap and holds both ends in her left hand as her cunt can wait no longer to be touched. Her right hand hungrily yanks up her skirt right up over her bum and hooks it in her waistband. She sits on her crouching heels and spreads her knees as far as she can, all the while pulling and releasing the scarf and licking her lips. The fragrance of her wet pussy drifts up to her face and it makes her desperate. She pulls her panties hard to the side and pauses for a moment to look at the sight before her. A dishevelled horny woman stares back at her with sex in her eyes. She watches as she dives her middle finger into her pussy and brings it out to rub on to her clit. Everything is wet, soaking wet, and she puts two fingers either side of her aching bud and massages, softly at first, then faster and harder. Her breathing quickens and she keeps in rhythm, pulsing the pressure on her throat in time with her finger fucking. Before she has time to catch herself she hears footsteps.

'Are you all right in there?' It is Debbie, the assistant.

'Yes fine, really.'

'It's just you sound like you're having an asthma attack or something.'

'No, please I'm fine; I'll just be a minute.' The thought of nearly being caught, or actually being caught heightens Selena's want and she releases the strap around her neck. It drops to the floor as she takes her pussy with both hands clenching them in with her thighs trying to apply as much pressure as she can. She holds her breath and crouches stock still and alert, terrified and exhilarated at the thought of Debbie pulling back the curtain. The air is so thick and electric around her she can hear the static deep in her ear canal. She needs to gasp. She needs to gulp in air but she is sure Debbie is still there. She silently grinds her mound into her fists and rubs hard either side of her clit.

It isn't enough.

She looks at the wild look in her own eyes and rises up with her back pressing the wall. Her eye make-up is smeared over her cheeks and her lipstick makes her mouth look raw. She looks like a woman that just needs to fuck. She can't stand it any longer. She releases her lungful of air in a huge wanton sigh and makes a decision. With a dramatic sweep she pulls back the curtain ready to present herself to the waiting assistant. The changing room is empty. For a moment, Selena can't decide if she is relieved or disappointed.

She closes the curtain and turns back to face the

mirror. She presses herself against her own reflection and uses all of her bodyweight to press her mound onto her hands. She can see her breath misting up the mirror as she pushes two fingers inside herself. In and out, in and out, she rocks her hips, sliding her cunt on and off her sticky long fingers. Harder and harder she pushes until she can hear her jawbone and pelvis banging against the mirror. Her orgasm surges and she groans until at last her fingers get sucked deeper in with the force of her pulsing come.

'Thank fuck for that.' She breathes on to the glass and wills herself to stand up properly. She stares at herself with wobbling legs and flushed face, hair sticking to her forehead and smiles.

'Are you sure you're OK?' the concerned-looking Debbie asks as Selena wobbles past.

'Yes I'm fine, really.' She smiles as she passes her the shirt. 'This is too small. I'll be taking this though.' She holds up the velvet scarf like a trophy and makes her way to the checkout.

He knew she had been up to something by the way her eyes looked up before she answered any of his questions. She held her hands clasped behind her and bit her lip coquettishly. He half expected if he looked at her feet they would be turned in and twisting about like a child lying badly.

'So where have you been?' He winced at the tone, he knew he sounded accusatory, there was just something about this woman that made him feel like she would dart off at any minute – go wherever her pussy led her, after all, that was how they met. He tried to smooth off the edges of the question, 'I mean, it's horrible outside, I was worried.'

'So you should be worried, I was lost without your big

strong presence. Who knows where I could have ended up?' She cocked her head and looked up through her hair at him.

'What do you mean?' He was getting nervous of his own envy and felt his skin redden, out of his control. 'What have you done?'

Selena brought her hand out from behind her back and held it on her delicate outstretched arm. Jim looked at the black scarf dangling from her fingers. She was once again swaying with a devious, no, naughty look on her face. That's it, thought Jim, she wants me to think she's been up to something. He stood up to his full height and breadth and towered over her.

'Just what is that you're holding, young lady?'

'Nothing.' She quickly whisked her hand behind her back and whimpered a nervous giggle. He reached behind her and grabbed her wrist.

'I said, show me.' He yanked her arm round with force and she gasped. 'What is this?' Jim snatched the scarf with his other hand while he kept a firm grip on her wrist. Her breathing was deep and heady and her eyelids flickered. She was fucking loving this. 'Where did you get this?' he demanded, using a strict voice.

'I took it.' Her eyes widened and he tightened the grip of her wrist.

'What do you mean you "took" it?'

'I stole it from a shop.' He pulled her into him, to let her feel his cock stirring in his jeans. She trembled and bit her lip again.

'So, you obviously need punishing, young lady.' Jim took the scarf from her and examined it. It was crushed and warm from being clutched in her hot sweaty hand. 'Come with me.' He was quite pleased with his authoritarian tone and it had the right effect on Selena who followed him meekly, a far cry from the demanding sexual goddess she'd been the night before. He like this surprising change and decided to take full advantage of this opportunity to dominate.

She stood next to the bed.

'What are you doing over there? Come here.' She took too long and he dragged her by both wrists to the bottom of the bed. 'Since you stole this, you will be punished with it.' He took the velvet strap and roughly bound it around her arms and yanked her forward towards the end of the bed. It was a classic brass frame and she had to lean over as he tied her on to the lowest bar. He liked her pose. Her high heels made her stick her ass out to balance and her back arched making her tits look amazing.

'Do you have anything to say for yourself?' Selena began to turn her face towards him. 'Keep your eyes down, you will not look me.' She returned her head and began to speak.

'I …'

'Shut up!' Jim stopped her, grabbed her hair and leaned into her ear. 'I'm not interested in what you've got to say,' he hissed, then released her head with a nudge.

He looked at her round ass straining through her skirt and smoothed his hand over it. He stood to the side of her and took her hair in his left hand again while rubbing her backside.

'Jim …' He heard her tiny voice and his reflex was to spank her, he did. She gasped and he knew she wanted it harder.

'I …' Smack.

'Said …' Smack.

'Shut …' Smack.

'The …' Smack.

'Fuck …' Smack.

'Up!' He really smacked her hard and the noise left a satisfying slap noise echoing through the room. He worried he might be taking it a bit far as he saw her panting but he caught a glimpse of her lips curl into a grin as she sneaked a look up at him. It made him hard to think she thought she was in control of this. She really was a filthy little madam who wanted fucking every way he could imagine. The future stretched out before him and so did his solid prick. He slid his hand to the hem of her skirt and ran his palm up her thigh.

Stockings and suspenders, no panties. She'd fucking planned it. He curled his fingers into the thick elastic and let it go. She jumped as it snapped back into place. He yanked the skirt up over her reddening ass and examined his work. It had been hard and she had taken it all with delight. Her ass was burning as he rubbed his hand over it and down into her crack. Her pussy was soaking and glistened looking as red and hot as her slapped bottom. He pulled his dick out of his jeans in one swift motion slid it deep into the heat of her wetness. He felt the walls of her pussy twitch around him and knew she was on the brink. He pulled out and watched with pleasure as she followed his retreat with her ass. He wanted her to be on fire.

She was moaning and grinding her thighs together curling her knees back and forth over each other in desperation.

'Please, Jim, for God's sake …'

'That's enough.' He placed one hand over her mouth while taking himself in the other. 'Is this what you want?' She nodded as he drew his hand up and down the length of his thick prick. Her face strained towards him and she licked her lips. He ran the tip of his head over her lips and her tongue darted over it. He let out a groan as her teeth parted, willing him to let her taste him. He moved forward and she sucked his cock into her mouth hard. She was hungry for him. Her mouth enveloped him and he raked his fingers into her hair and pulled in deeper. Again and again she slid her burning tongue and teeth down his shaft, deeper every time. He could feel her increasing the force, ramming him into her throat and he was ready to explode. He grabbed a fistful of her hair and yanked her head back.

'That's enough!' Jim withdrew and watched her full lips pout and softly smack together. He ran his hands down her arms and impulsively tightened the strapping around her wrists. Her hands were turning white with the pressure and he started to loosen them off.

'No!' Selena's hair was stuck to her flushed cheeks and a wisp had found its way into the corner of her mouth. She motioned to her bindings, 'leave it!' Jim retied the strap and watched as Selena tried to get rid of the hair by first blowing it, then using her tongue. Jim could tell it was irritating her and smiled. He placed his hand back on her ass and slowly traced his palm up over the fabric of her skirt straining over her buttocks.

At the waist band, he pulled out her blouse and ran his hands round her middle and up to her breasts. She shivered and he eased the top of her bra down releasing her turgid nipples. They gently bounced and he squeezed the swollen mounds together, massaging the hard nipples between his finger and thumb. She was grinding her hips and ass again into thin air and Jim could smell her frustration. He took his hands away and gently tugged the hair from her lip and cheek.

His cock was aching, it was getting too much for him to resist and he took his position behind Selena once again. Her hips thrust backwards into him and he spread her buttocks apart with both hands. He couldn't wait any longer and thrust right into her, jamming his pelvis into her ass cheeks. They both groaned, pussy and cock twitching and bucking. He pulled out slowly and dived back in. It was hot and soft and luscious and his dick had never felt so slick. As he kept on sliding himself in and out of her engorged pussy he reached around to her ripe clit and she gasped as he rubbed it with his soaking fingers.

They fucked harder and harder until the surge of come was too much and Jim slammed himself into the very centre of Selena. She let out a shriek as he shot his love deep into her twitching pussy and they slid to the floor together panting.

Later, as Selena gently folds the scarf and puts it away, she takes the receipt from her purse and quietly throws it in the bin with a small smile.

You're My Toy
by Sommer Marsden

It was the damnedest Christmas present I had ever seen. I pulled it out, held it up in all its blue silicone glory. 'What in the world?'

Aaron smiled and blushed. 'It's for you.'

'To wear?'

'No, it's for me to wear and for you to ...'

'To?'

'Benefit from.' He laughed.

I could smell that new plastic smell, like lawn chairs or flip-flops, and I'd be a liar if I didn't admit that my pussy went wet when I looked at it. 'So when I get angry and call you a fuck-face you take me seriously?'

'Let me do it.' His hand crept up my thigh. All around us wrapping and ribbons and bows.

'Soon.' It made me nervous. I admit it. I wasn't sure why, but it almost seemed unfair to Aaron.

'Janie, Janie,' he sighed, climbing onto me, he pushed my thighs wide with his big knee and pushed his warm hands into my pyjama bottoms. His fingers slipped over my clit and then into me with such ease. I was so wet already. 'Don't you get it?'

'I think I'm about to,' I said, and then he kissed me quiet.

He tugged at my jammie bottoms, his mouth a wet trail from my lips to my belly button to my pussy. Hot perfect swirls of his tongue had me clutching the shiny silver wrapping and arching up to meet his mouth. 'I want to do it. It's a present for me as much as for you. This way I'll be your toy.'

'I think I can deal with that.' I shut my eyes as he sucked my clit, pushing the flat of his tongue to my moist pussy. Aaron arched his rigid tongue into my cunt, fucking my pussy with his mouth only until I hauled him up by his hair, my shaking fingers twined in his dark locks. 'I will think it over while we ...'

I spread my legs further, willing him to push his dick inside me, begging him with my movements to fuck me senseless.

'Bang like monkeys? Fuck like animals? Do the nasty?' Aaron laughed as he plunged into me, his hard cock tripping all the bundles of nerves deep inside me that made me pant like a dog while I came.

'Yes, yes, and yes!' I wrapped my legs around his flanks, pulling him into my pussy deeper so that the head of his cock pushed my g-spot.

Aaron decided to play dirty. He took a bright blue ribbon from the floor and tied me to the back of his mother's antique chair. Heavy dark wood carved with smiling moons and shooting stars. The thing weighed a ton and I was powerless to get at him. He pulled free of me as my body vibrated with urgency. I was right there on the crisp paper edge of coming and he was leaving me!

'Now listen, I don't want to rush you. And I don't want to push you.' He kissed my lips and I tasted my own juices on his mouth. He pushed his tongue deeper so that it was like sucking his cock. He nibbled my throat, my collar bone and my belly button before capturing a nipple in his mouth and sucking hard. The tug on my breast echoed in my cunt. A hollow sucking sensation that had me testing that damn ribbon and jerking the heavy wooden chair in a jittery dance.

'OK, fine, don't push me! Fuck me! It's Christmas! I need it,' I was at the point of begging and I simply didn't care.

'Let me do it then. Let me wear the strap on and fuck you until you cry,' he said, his mouth covering my vulva again, licking the sweet sticky juices of my need from my body. I tossed my hips at him like I was on a ship and begged.

'Please, oh fuck, please. Whatever you want.'

'Tomorrow? You'll let me do it tomorrow?'

'Yes, yes! Baby Jesus, merry Christmas, yes!' I shouted and pushed my pussy higher to him.

'Thanks, Rits. I love you baby. You're the best,' he laughed, kissing me so hard my scalp prickled from rug burn.

Aaron shoved his big hands under my ass cheeks, hoisting me a bit higher and angling me perfectly. When he shoved into me, balls deep and brisk, little purple and pink sparkles exploded in my vision. Five hard strokes, like he was driving nails or jack hammering concrete and I came, biting his shoulder so hard he growled. 'Don't make me bleed, Janie!' But he fucked me faster still, inching all three of us (me, him and the heavy antique chair) across the living room floor. When he finally came, we lay tangled and panting half under the Christmas tree. The chair had knocked off a few bulbs and a string of lights dangled like drunks after a long party.

'Tomorrow?'

He was all gentleness and butterfly kisses then. His fingers dancing over my skin so softly I shivered. I eyed the box and the somehow brutal looking dildo erected from the face harness. Part of it scared the shit out of me and part of it made my cunt beat with an eager wet pulse. I nodded.

'Tomorrow,' I agreed.

All the next day I worried about it. Even when I answered the phone at work, in my head would be a big blue dildo on a black face mask. I could see Aaron coming at me, on hands and knees. A huge fake hard-on in front of him. I shook my head, trying to focus on what my customer was saying. But then my mind would switch it up. Me spread eagle against the basement wall, Aaron on his knees coming at me from behind. Fucking ms slow and sure and then fast and frantic with the bright plasticine dick.

'What?' I stammered. Three people hung up on me and my boss asked me if I'd had enough sleep.

I'd had plenty of sleep. I'd had sleep and sex all night long. Just the thought of using the toy on me had Aaron raring to go. Our whole evening had been spent in some form of debauchery or other. He had run me a strawberry scented bubbled bath and then run through our entire collection of toys. Rubbing my pussy and my tender clit with first the red marbled vibrator, then purple, then blue and then green. Who knew that we had such a rainbow's array of fake cocks in our house?

He had eaten my pussy until I babbled and then, giddy, exhausted and beyond coming again, I turned over and offered him my ass. Aaron had talked dirty the entire time. A fantasy-fuelled energized rabbit whose drum to bang happened to be, 'I'm going to fuck you so good, baby. I'm your toy. Say it, Janie. Say it, baby.'

'You're my toy,' I sighed, head down, body twisted in a pain pleasure combo as my loving husband spanked my ass and fucked me hard. He came, balls deep, holding onto my hips for dear life, coming into my back door.

Work was too much, I had to get home. I couldn't focus. My boss sent me out early. And there he was. Already home, already prepping. Flowers and candles and food galore. Fuck Face.

'I couldn't concentrate,' I confessed.

'Me neither.'

'I came home.'

'Me, too. Janie?'

He looked worried and my heart twisted a little. 'Yeah, baby?'

'You don't think it's too dirty, do you? It doesn't freak you out, does it?'

I touched the evident bulge in his dust covered blue jeans. A mistake at work on a construction site could cost someone life or limb, I was glad he came home. 'No, Aaron. I think it's just dirty enough. So dirty, I could barely keep my head on straight. You've fucked me 60 different ways in that face harness today. In my head, but still ...'

'And I want to do it for real. Now.' His hands were down in my pants, pushing into my cunt. Intrusive but in the best possible way. He invaded me with his big warm digits until I sank back against the counter, legs splayed like a fuck slut. My hands rubbed the length of his hard cock and I listened to him panting in a nearly desperate way. One of my favourite sounds in the world – out-of-his-mind-horny man.

'That would be good,' I laughed. He had my pants tangled down around my ass and my panties got caught. Aaron grabbed a paring knife from the counter and slit the sides –one, two easy as pie. He pushed the whole mess of clothing to the side and got on his knees. I watched him rub his hard pole through his pants and my eyelids sank down. I wanted him naked doing that.

'What?' His mouth pressed to me, his tongue wetting me perfectly. My clit, so swollen he could nibble on it, screamed for more.

'Take off your clothes. Do that naked. I like to watch you jack off.' I blushed when I said it, but I said it anyway. He was out of his clothes and digging under the tree as I unbuttoned my work blouse and unhooked my bra. I stood, shivering with goose bumps in the chilly kitchen.

When he came back, he held the face harness out to me and kneeled back down. His flushed hard-on poker straight from his slim hips, a glistening dot of pre-come rested on the swollen head. He sank himself face first into my pussy and resumed eating me out until I was absentmindedly rubbing the fake cock in my hands like a worry stone.

'Ready?' He smiled up at me. He had intended to get me so horny and on edge that I couldn't give the face piece a second thought. And I didn't. I looked at it now and saw a big blue orgasm clutched in my hand.

'Ready.' I bent and strapped it on him. Aaron's hands trembled over the length of his dick, pumping so that he was close to purple and I knew from years of marriage, so close to coming a sneeze would set him off. 'Fuck me, Aaron.'

He sighed behind the mask and leaned in, shoving the appendage before him. My mind conjured up all things dirty and perverse: Unicorn horns; a Cyclops with a penis for an eye; riding a bike with a dildo seat. I shook my head. What was I thinking? But then I wasn't. He was shoving into me, his head going back and forth like he was giving a blow job. An inverted blow job. He was fucking me with his mouth and the cobalt blue dick that sprouted from between his lips.

I sprawled backwards on the counter, hips banging the grey granite workspace. Aaron stood, the protrusion on his face slippery with my juices. He pushed his hands under my ass, levering me up until I lay splayed on the cool surface, legs wide for him. He delved back in, hands encircling my ankles like flesh and blood cuffs. He fucked me hard, his head pistoning back and forth as I watched, mesmerized. I came, flooding his face and the leather tethers with wet sticky fluid. 'God, oh, God. Another. I want another.' Seeing him there, that way just for me was too much. I rolled to the side, pushing Aaron, 'Go, go, get on the counter.' I pushed at him. He arranged himself lengthwise on the counter like a patient on a hospital bed. My pussy quaked at seeing him that way, his permanent facial erection high and hard and waiting for me.

Aaron remained mute behind the fitted face piece. I couldn't see his mouth, but could tell from the laugh lines around his eyes that he was smiling. His hand pistoned along the length of his cock and I dropped down, sucking him into my mouth frantically. I swallowed his dick and inhaled deeply through my nose to let him into my throat. All of him filled my throat and the rich smell of sex filled my nose. I cradled his balls in my hands, stroking him from dick to asshole until he mewled softly behind his mask. He fucked my mouth, his movements jittery, the reverse of what he'd just done to me. When he thrust too fast, I stilled him with my hand. 'No more. Wait.'

I crawled so that my pussy hovered over his face. I ran the smooth blue head of the cock over my dripping hole and locked eyes with Aaron. 'Do you want me to fuck your face, Aaron? Do you?'

Aaron nodded, his eyes sparkling with excitement and need. A muffled mmph passed for a yes.

I slid the head only into my wet pussy and locked my

legs, my knees brushing the cool unforgiving stone. Aaron jerked his head up to thrust, his fist sliding up and down his rock hard dick. I levered up and away from him.

'Be a good boy or I won't let you. I'll leave you here hard and desperate and go back to work. Now that I've come I bet I can concentrate better.'

I was lying through my teeth, but he let his neck relax as he stroked his shaft and pleaded with his eyes.

I put the head back in, lowering inch by bright blue inch so that my thighs covered his ears and my cunt covered the phallus and Aaron's face. His hand flew over his erection, his hips thrusting up eagerly to the rhythm of his own sliding palm. I rode the face mask slow and sure. To make him suffer and to get him off. It was a win, win situation.

I gripped the edge of the counter, struggling to keep my composure and failing. I raised and lowered my hips, so fast, fucking myself with Aaron's extra cock that I thought I might smother him. I knew I hadn't when he reached up with a hand and gathered some of my juices on his finger. His other hand jacked his dick furiously, his knees coming up, feet pounding the counter. I pushed back and Aaron pushed his thick finger into my ass, slow and steady the way I like. He added a second as I slammed down over and over. Finally coming in a rush of words and wetness.

I turned to see the thick spurts of pearly come sliding over his banged up knuckles, his dusty fingers, his perfect big fist.

I rested my head on the stone, trying to imagine what could be done with such a toy.

When I got the mask off of Aaron to kiss him, and kiss him I did, he solved the mystery.

'Tomorrow, meet me at Christine's after work.'

I got off at 3.00, he got off at 3.30. 'A bit early for dinner,' I muttered, licking the perfect sweet taste of my pussy off his lips.

'Not for dinner. Just for coffee. And for me.'

'You?'

'I'm going under the table.'

My knees were weak.

I actually thought I would pass out walking into Christine's. We'd been there a thousand times it seemed, but not with an agenda. The skirt that Aaron had picked out so carefully, swung and swished over my thigh high stockings. The hem kissed my tall black boots. As for panties, though, nothing but breeze. I was bare under the charcoal grey sheath skirt and my pussy begged for more attention from my man. I smiled to myself, fought the clawing anxiety over getting caught and walked into dark restaurant.

The light was always set to ambient due to Christine's reputation as being the romantic eatery. The host found me and seated me at table three. 'The gentleman was here,' he said frowning. 'He must have excused himself for a moment. Can I get the lady a drink?'

Already a warm, heavy hand had curled around my stocking clad ankle. Another one was sliding up my inner calf with a whisper of nylon, a masculine unseen presence that left me trembling. I swallowed hard, smiled. 'I would love a nice big wine. Emphasis on the word big,' I joked. The waiter frowned again but scampered off.

Aaron had pushed my skirt up above my knees so it puddled around my hips. I felt the smooth cool dildo slide along the slit of my pussy lips. I splayed my legs, biting the tip of my tongue to at least maintain a semblance of control. He nudged my opening with the tip of his tool

51

and I slid a bit lower in my seat. My pulse slammed heavily in my ears and I was finding it hard to swallow even my own spit. Dizzy and horny and excited, I arched up to meet him just a bit and he slipped the cock home inside my moist hole.

'Oh, God.'

The server set my wine down and gave me a quizzical look. My fingers were twisted in the white linen table cloth and I could feel the twin spots of cherry red on my cheeks. 'Oh, God ... that looks really, really good,' I managed.

He smiled, still looking wary of me. 'Yes, well, would you care to wait for the gentleman or can I get you ...'

'I'll wait! I'll wait,' I sighed, because Aaron had slammed the bright blue dildo home. He pushed, craning the whole of his face forward to rub my g-spot with is new favourite toy. 'Jesus. I. Will. Wait.'

The host blinked and backed away from me. His eyes ping-ponged across the room for Aaron. God, I wondered what would happen if they found Aaron under there? That way. Big blue rod strapped to his face, fucking his wife under the table like a whore? What would happen?

I'll tell you what did happen. I came at the thought. I came, biting my tongue, clenching my jaw and my wine glass. I waited for the delicate crystal stem to shatter, but it didn't. I waited for Aaron to stop, but he didn't.

He kept fucking me.

I took a swig of wine and our actual waiter appeared. 'Hi, I'm Ed and I'll be your ... are you OK?'

Aaron had my thighs pinned wide in the ladder back chair. One of my hands gripped my butter knife, no clue why, and the other the edge of the seat for balance. He had the long fake dick buried deep in my pussy by then and he was swirling it. Great looping motions that managed to trip every good nerve I possessed. His fingers pressed and stroked over my clit and I held my breath until spots appeared in my vision. Fingers on my swollen button, fingers probing my ass, and his face swishing and whirling that blue monstrosity deep into the wet well of my cunt.

'I am fine!' I crowed as I came, a long unwinding orgasm that for some reason set me to laughing. Maybe it was the venue. Maybe it was the release.

I heard the slapping frantic sounds of my wonderful, polite, upstanding husband beating off under the table like a common john and a blip of pleasure rolled through my pelvis. A little amused bouche of an orgasm. I heard a muffled grunt and sigh as hot, sticky come splashed on my thighs and knees. He was painting me.

This waiter was adorable. I saw his eyes take in just the heel of Aaron's boot. He was on to us. I heard the jingle jangle of the harness's rings and felt it drop at my feet.

'If the lady and gentlemen would like some more time, I can come back.' He had backed up three steps, our waiter. Back far enough for me to see the exquisite hard-on tenting his plain black server pants. I ran my tongue over my bottom lip.

There was another fantasy that Aaron and I had discussed ... a third party.

'No. I think we're good,' Aaron said, plopping into his chair. His hair stood up in whirls and horns and his face was flushed and slightly damp by his lips. That was me on his face. I shivered.

'Very well. Can I get you an appetizer?'

'Another one?' Aaron joked.

I laughed. Our waiter crept closer, sharing our secret, somehow drawn by it. He leaned in close, order pad in hand. 'I'm sure very little could top that one,' he said, eyes darting to me and then my husband.

Aaron grinned. His hand found my thigh under the table where my skirt still rode high around my hips. I knew he was thinking what I was thinking. 'So, Ed, would you be offended if someone called you fuck face?' my man whispered. 'And how are you at the whole sharing thing? Are you a good sharer, Ed?'

Ed was smiling but I was more focused on the bulge in his trousers and the mental image I had of him sporting a big blue cock from his pretty boy face.

I liked my new toy. I liked it a lot.

Date Night
by Ariel Graham

The first time I met him, he was looking for his wife's cat. The neighbourhood was new, and so were all the residents, and seeing we were a commute away from San Francisco and almost everyone seemed to drive into the city daily, after several months we were all still getting acquainted and learning names.

Mine's Charlene, but I didn't know his, and we'd been living a very short distance apart for a lot of months. What I did know was that he and his wife both worked, car pooled or park-and-ride shared with other groups, and kept late hours, barbecued on weekends, and didn't have any obvious kids.

Now I also knew they had a cat. That, or the male half of the couple was in serious need of therapy, because he was walking bent double, peering under cars and calling someone or something named Mr Chips.

I had just gotten out of my car and was unloading the groceries when Mr Chips' human came face to mid-thigh with me, and stopped dead. I watched the blush move up his face from the open collar of his chambray work shirt and thought I kind of liked it. The guy was dark, the kind of dark that shaves twice a day or ends up pirate-swarthy. He had light eyes and a chipped front tooth that showed when he grinned. I grinned back and stuck out my hand.

'Charlene Evers,' I told him. 'Please tell me you're

looking for a cat.'

His blush deepened a little. 'Cory Phillips. I think we're neighbours.'

'Definitely,' I said, nodding at our house. Tiny yard, cement walkway. The eaves on our houses almost touched, upstairs bedroom windows maybe 15 feet apart. 'Would you like a hand in looking for – was it Mr Chips?'

He looked even more embarrassed, if possible, which led me to believe it was his wife's cat.

'He won't come to anyone else,' he said, as if this were a failing on his, or the cat's, part.

'Really?' I handed him one of my grocery bags so I could rummage inside it. 'I have a way with cats,' I said, and produced a pop-top single-serve-sized can of tuna.

Cory laughed.

I put the can down mid-sidewalk and Cory called. About 30 seconds later a sleek black cat with white whiskers and a white moustache appeared from my back yard, looked at me with brief suspicion, ignored Cory and tucked into the tuna.

'And now he's eaten your lunch,' Cory said, stooping to pet the cat.

'No worries. Frees me up to have pizza.'

'I saw you talking to the neighbour,' Vince said when I went inside. He stood inside the living room, far enough back he couldn't be seen through the narrow floor-to-ceiling window next to the front door which comprised our entire view from the front of the house except for one lone window in what had become our spare room.

'You should have come out,' I said and plopped the carryalls on the counter. My job was to shop if we didn't want to live on potato chips and mac-n-cheese out of a box. His job was to put everything away.

Vince shrugged and stooped to give me a kiss. I brushed his blond feathery hair back and stood on tiptoe to meet him halfway.

'I liked watching the two of you together. You looked good, your blonde hair and him so dark.'

I grinned. I'd fallen half in lust with our neighbour on first sight but it was pretty obvious nothing was going to come of it. 'Don't get your hopes up,' I said. 'He nearly passed out from embarrassment just talking to me.'

I flipped the under cabinet lights on and started paging through a cookbook looking for something fast, easy and to which I had all the ingredients without going back to the grocery.

'So you mean it's unlikely he's going to be doing any of this?' Vince asked and came up behind me, slipping his arms over mine and reaching around to cup and squeeze my breasts. I let the cookbook pages rifle closed and leaned back against him. We could always get take-out.

'Mm, I don't think so.'

'How about this?' he asked, and ran his hands down the front of my body until he cupped my sex in his hand.

'Mm. Oh God. No. I think that would embarrass him.'

'Shame, that,' Vince said. He pulled the snap on my jeans, let the zip down and started tugging until my jeans and thong came down to my knees. He lifted me then, still facing the counter, and doubled me over the tile. One hand pressed down on the small of my back. The other dipped down and two fingers slid into me.

Vince moaned. 'You're so wet. I want to watch him do this to you.'

I felt him move slightly away and knew he was watching as his own fingers disappeared inside me, pretending someone else was finger-fucking me.

'Don't stop,' I said, and the hand on my back went

57

away. I heard him fumbling wrong-handed with his own clothing and then he moved in close again, pushing his cock up where his fingers had been, moving my body so my clit ground against the tile, painful and intense. I arched up under him and Vince said, 'I just. Want to watch. Someone else. Fuck you.' And came inside me even as I started to come.

Dinner ended up being pizza. Now I really was going to have to replace that tuna.

We went upstairs late that night, still content from pizza and sex, carrying our books. Vince went into the bedroom first so he could cross the dark expanse and turn on the bedside light rather than the overhead. I paused so I could turn off the hall light and was partway across the bedroom when he gestured me to be still.

'What?' I asked, though I dutifully froze in place.

'Come look.'

Across from us, separated by maybe 15 feet, Cory's bedroom was lit softly with candles. I squinted and an instant later I saw what Vince was watching.

Cory's cock was long and obviously very hard and he stood with his legs spread wide, in profile to the window, his head thrown back and one hand on his wife's head where she knelt, naked and golden, one hand cupping his balls as she sucked him off. Her other hand moved fast between her own legs.

I stood without moving, unwilling to look away, and felt Vince come up behind me, wrapping himself around me again. I was afraid to move, afraid we'd be seen, but Vince tugged my clothes, making me shift and turn within his grasp while across from us Cory's wife continued sucking and playing.

Vince got me naked and pushed me forward, just

enough he could bend his knees, his long legs on either side of mine, and shove his cock hard into my cunt. I moaned, my own hands moving to find my clit as Vince reached around me to squeeze my nipples, and some movement we made caught Cory's attention. He stilled, frowning toward our window, and I wasn't sure if we were far enough back from the light that he'd see us but I tried to go still. Vince hadn't noticed, maybe, and he took up a rhythm then, slamming into me and I looked away for just an instant. When I looked back Cory's head was thrown back, mouth open, his cock spurting on to his wife's breasts. She had her mouth open and her own hand had stilled, fingers probably still sunk deep inside herself.

I slipped over the edge, then, Vince coming hard inside me again, and when I looked up again, Cory's windows were closed, the curtains drawn.

For the next week I studiously avoided my neighbours. Vince, for all that he talks a good game and really would like to see me somewhere else with someone else, is shy. I didn't ask him about it, but he didn't say anything about Cory, so I figured he was doing a little subtle reconnaissance before leaving the house too. But just because I took care when going out to my car to drive to the humane society where I worked telling people that yes, little fluffy kittens did cost a lot to adopt, but look how *cute*, just because I watched on my way in and out of the house didn't mean I didn't look over at their bedroom windows every time I passed by ours.

Their curtains stayed closed.

'I'm going to be late tonight,' Vince said as we got ready for work a week after the inadvertent adventure.

That always sucks.

'How come?' Working at the humane society is a

much easier dress code than working for an architectural firm. I was dressed long before Vince and sitting on the bed watching him.

'Just client meetings. Law firm wants to renovate a downtown building.' He stopped fussing with his tie – he couldn't tie them worth a damn and neither could I, so often he skipped it, got frowned at by the older partners but spent the day breathing easier – and came over to put his arms around me. 'If I found you naked and waiting when I got home –'

I nipped at his chin. 'Been there, done that. Your ETA had no bearing on reality. I was cold, tired and doing a crossword.'

He nodded, remembering. 'We had boxed mac-n-cheese and watched a talk show. We *are* sexy.'

I laughed. 'Just call me if you're going to be too late,' and we both headed out.

I wasn't sure if it was my imagination but I thought he took a brief look around before he went outside.

Vince wasn't home when I got home, or when I finished doing a load of laundry or later when I pulled together everything we'd need for dinner, so I decided to take a run. Just after seven, it was still light and I ran along one of the green belts the city provided. Everyone said they were dangerous but there were so many joggers, runners, walkers, dog walkers, bikers, skaters and lovers that the only danger was traffic congestion, not being pulled into the foliage and attacked.

The sun was collapsing into a hot red disk over the Bay when I got back to our neighbourhood. I slowed half a block out, walking, and a few houses away I saw Vince. He always looked so good to me, tall and tanned and lean, sleeves rolled up to his elbows and the lanky, confident

way he stood. I was about to call out to him when I saw
he was talking to someone and I slowed. A few steps
closer and I saw he and Cory stood talking. Both were in
profile to me, Vince light and Cory dark, both tall and
handsome. I thought about what Vince always wanted and
shivered a little. Then I thought about what had happened
a week ago and started thinking about crossing back to the
far side of the street and taking a few more laps around
the block until Cory went away.

Vince spotted me and called me over. 'You two have
met, right?'

I'm blonde. I get red faced when I run. At least they
couldn't tell I was blushing. Probably. 'Nice to see you
again,' I said. 'How's Mr Chips?'

'Arrogant,' Cory said and I noticed he looked a little
red faced himself. 'Anyway, Vince, nice meeting you.
Ten o'clock?'

'Ten o'clock,' Vince agreed.

'What's at ten o'clock?' I asked, and both men gave
me blank expressions.

'I'll give the cat your regards,' Cory said and went
away.

'Vince?'

He was already heading inside.

'Yes?' He held the door open for me.

'What's ten o'clock?'

'A time of day.'

'You're hilarious.'

'Can't help it.'

We'd stopped inside the doorway. Vince now gave me
a long look. 'You look awful.'

'Thank you. And there I was admiring you when I got
back from my run.'

'And Cory?'

I shrugged. 'I don't know if he likes admiring you or not.'

Vince rolled his eyes. 'You know what I mean.'

I winked. 'Fair play. What's at ten o'clock?'

'If you really want to know, you'll have to bribe me.'

I gave him a look. He unzipped his pants. I'm never averse to a bit of bribery. We moved off the tiled entryway and I knelt, drew his hard, thick cock into my mouth and nearly choked when Vince took up a very fast, deep rhythm. Something had him very happy to see me.

When he got close, I pulled back and grinned up at him. 'What's at ten o'clock?'

He looked at me with mock exasperation. 'Wench. Fine. Sex with the neighbours.'

And he slid his hard, straining cock back into my astonished, open mouth.

I pestered him through dinner, and cleanup, and during my own clean-up from my run, though eventually Vince just got tired of avoiding answering my questions and left the bathroom and left me to shower alone.

By eight o'clock I was a bundle of nerves. By nine o'clock I'd cleaned nearly everything in the house, even though I was wearing a pretty loose skirt and a tank top and no underwear per Vince's rather stringent suggestion.

Just before ten o'clock I'd decided it might be a good idea to pack everything we owned and move to another house. Vince's fantasy had been exciting as a fantasy. The reality a week earlier had been exciting as accidental reality. But tonight had a plan and Vince wouldn't tell me what it was. My heartbeat was loud and fast in my ears and I felt dizzy and off balance.

'And you call me the shy one,' Vince said as ten o'clock rolled around and we were still sitting alone in our living room.

I wouldn't have admitted it for anything in the world but I was a little disappointed that we were still home, and still alone together.

'I didn't know you knew I think you're shy,' I said.

Vince worked his way through my sentence and added, 'And you also consider me the unobservant one?'

Since he'd already tripped over several very apparent objects left out on the floor and asked me three times where his book was when it was on the coffee table in front of him, I thought I could nod at that one.

I didn't. I was still nervous. 'It's ten o'clock,' I said finally. 'After.' I nodded at the clock on the DVD player before I remembered it often ran fast.

'You're right. *Very* observant.' And he smirked, and held his hand out, and I swallowed and stood and took it, wondering.

He led me upstairs. There was something comforting knowing we were still in our own house. There was something wildly exciting about knowing the little I did – soon we wouldn't be alone in our house. Were they coming over? Were we changing and going over there? What had Cory and Vince agreed to?

And halfway up the stairs I thought I understood. Sex with the neighbours. We'd already had sex with the neighbours, hadn't we? And while maybe Vince hadn't watched Cory actually touching me, it had been *very good* sex between us that night.

The bedroom light was already on. The bedside lights had been moved and faced each other in the middle of the room, illuminating a spot directly across from the side windows. The back windows drapes were closed. The side windows drapes stood open, damp Bay air coming in the window and the low sound of voices from across the short distance between our houses.

Cory and his wife – Anna, Vince said she was called – stood framed in a similar glow of light within their own bedroom.

She was small and honey coloured, with a mane of hair and lips so glossed they glistened in the light. She wore a simple black dress with white buttons all the way down the front and she stood holding Cory's hand. Cory wore jeans, no shirt, his face well past its mandatory five o'clock shave. I wanted to bridge the distance between us and lick the coarse stubble on his chin. I wanted to run my fingers over his wife's breasts and tear the black dress from her.

But I couldn't touch them. So I turned to Vince and rose on tiptoe to wrap my arms around his neck and find his mouth with mine.

His mouth crushed my lips. He bit my lower lip and tugged. His hands found the hem of my dress and hauled it up. I felt cool air on my naked ass and Vince's hands, squeezing, long fingers pressing my flesh, lifting, moulding, mauling, separating. I moved a little, opened my eyes, and saw that Cory had unbuttoned Anna's dress down to her waist. Her breasts were as golden as the rest of her, with surprisingly pink nipples, hard and long. Cory turned her, trying to watch us at the same time he bit and licked. Anna's head fell back. She reached for him, fumbling with his jeans even as he pulled her dress the rest of the way open, showing us her slightly rounded stomach and shaved mons, the way she stood with her legs slightly apart, waiting for his hand or cock or mouth to find its way there.

I shuddered and tugged at Vince's shorts, even as he tangled me in my tank top, pulling it over my head, getting it into his face, laughing in joint frustration as we briefly blindfolded ourselves. And then we were watching again, watching as Cory knelt in front of Anna, his tongue working between her legs, her hands pressing and squeezing her own breasts, and Vince held me in front of him and a little to the side, my hand caressing his cock, his fingers spreading my juices.

At some signal I missed, or by some unspoken mutual agreement, we all stopped, both men crossing their respective rooms to bring back straight-backed chairs into the light and since the one in our room was one of our dining room chairs, I understood this had been arranged. Vince sat, and pulled me to him, turned me back to face the window where Cory and Anna had assumed the same poses. And then he pulled me down on his cock, his hands coming around to squeeze and play with my breasts.

'Spread your legs over mine,' he said, his voice hoarse, and I saw Anna straddling Cory, her sex splayed and Cory's cock sunk deep inside her. I threw my legs over Vince's and he pushed me forward, just enough so my shoulders moved away from him, my ass moved toward him and he sank deep into me, fucking me very fast.

We all came within minutes of each other. My usually silent partner made some kind of shout as he buried himself inside me and came. I don't think I made a sound, but Anna cried out Cory's name and Cory shouted something incoherent and I realised until then we'd all been mostly silent.

And stayed that way after. In the aftermath we sat, two plus two, wives still straddling husbands' laps, the four of us sweaty and dishevelled and sated, and stared at each other across the space between our houses.

Finally we all started moving and I expected someone

to draw the curtains and that perhaps all four of us would be avoiding the others for quite some time. Instead, when Vince and I stood and started to turn off the lights, at least the rather stage lights the bedside table lamps created, we saw a naked and beautiful Cory come up to the window with a notepad. We could have heard him easily if he'd spoken and raised his voice even a little, but somehow communicating through signs was in keeping with the evening.

Cory's sign read, 'Same time next week?'

Vince grinned at me, then rummaged until he found an old sketch pad and a marker and wrote on the back, 'It's a date.'

Splendide Girl
by Courtney James

I didn't take the job because of the uniform, gorgeous though it was. That was just a bonus. I took it because Michael Benington was offering me the chance to make a long-held dream come true.

When I read in the local paper that Benington was planning to re-open the Splendide, I was determined to get a job there. The cinema, opened in the late 1920s, had once been the most impressive building in town. Its Art Deco interior was decorated in rich shades of gold and red, and its bar was fitted out with gleaming bronze rails. The auditorium boasted a huge crystal chandelier and two rows of love seats right at the back, where couples could sit together in cosy comfort to watch the film – or not, as they chose. At the interval, a Wurlitzer organ would rise up through a trapdoor in the stage, and the audience would be entertained with a selection of popular tunes. I was taken there a few times when I was a child, and even though the once-plush seats were rather moth-eaten and the owner could no longer afford to employ an organist, I still thought it was the most magical place on earth. When I grew up, I told myself, I would work in that glorious picture palace.

Then a new shopping mall appeared on the edge of town. Among its many attractions was an eight-screen multiplex cinema. Even though most of the screens weren't much larger than the average front room, the Splendide couldn't compete with the choice it offered, and within a year it had been forced to close. It reopened briefly as a bingo hall, but the town centre as a whole was in decline, shoppers lured away by the delights of the mall, and soon the Splendide was boarded up and forgotten.

Michael Benington was determined to change that. An avowed cinema buff who had made his money in property development, he announced his plan to buy and run the Splendide. He intended to restore it to the beauty of its pre-war heyday, and once it was complete, he would be actively recruiting staff.

I watched as the boards came down and the builders moved in. Benington worked fast, and three months later I was one of almost a hundred people who applied to work at the Splendide. I'd like to think my genuine love for the building and my knowledge of film helped me land the job. In truth, it had as much to do with the fact I fitted Benington's vision of what a Splendide usherette should look like. In keeping with the cinema's beginnings, he planned to screen classic black-and-white movies alongside current releases and the subtitled art house films the multiplex never showed. He really wanted the audience to feel they were stepping back in time as they entered the cinema's beautifully restored foyer. This meant proper uniforms for the staff, rather than the drab polo shirts and casual slacks more usual elsewhere.

Benington had a sample usherette's uniform draped over a mannequin by his desk. It consisted of a short, fitted red jacket with gold buttons down the front, a tight skirt that came to mid-thigh level and a perky pillbox hat. It was, he told me, designed to be worn with high heels and stockings, not tights. Impractical but sexy, particularly when you were as short and busty as I was. With my cloud of curly red hair peeking from beneath the hat, I knew I would look like a pocket dynamo from a Busby Berkeley musical. He clearly realised that, too. 'You have all the attributes I'm looking for, Kirsty,' he said, a wickedly curving smile on his face. 'The job's yours if you want it.'

I wanted it very much, and a week later I was slipping into my uniform for the first time, ready to begin work as a Splendide girl. The clothes seemed to demand appropriate underwear beneath them, so I'd treated myself to a black bra, French-cut satin knickers and deep suspender belt with six straps from a vintage lingerie shop. As I hooked my seamed black stockings to the suspenders, I felt like a 40s siren, my hourglass curves defined and emphasised by the flattering underwear. Pulling the jacket and skirt over the top made me strangely horny, as though I was surrendering to a lover's caress. Looking at my reflection in the bedroom mirror, I couldn't resist the urge to smooth my hands over my body, following the sleek lines of my breasts and hips. Even though I knew I ran the risk of being late on my first day on the job, I gave in to the overwhelming impulse to lift my skirt and touch myself through my knickers. My pussy seemed to blossom as I stroked it, growing hotter and wetter by the moment.

In my mind, I was standing on the stage at the Splendide, with an audience of anonymous voyeurs revelling in my performance. Even though I couldn't see their faces, I knew each one, male and female, was rapt with lust, turned on by the sight of my fingers snaking into my underwear and up into my cunt. The screen was dark, the only spotlight on me as I frigged myself to a swift, breathless climax. In reality, my knees sagged and I clutched on to the mirror as I came. Taking a moment to clean myself up, I was soon out of the house and on my way with a wiggle in my walk, looking forward more than ever to starting work at the Splendide.

The glamour of the job wore off more quickly than I might have expected. It was fun to show cinema-goers to their seats with the aid of a cute little torch, and when I stood at the front of the auditorium with my tray of peanuts and ice creams, I never failed to get admiring looks and even blatant come-ons from my customers. I simply hadn't realised how even the most skilfully plotted, stylishly shot film could become tedious once you'd seen it six times in a row. If the film was bad to begin with – and many of them were – by the end of its run I was left feeling that I would rather claw my own eyes out than watch it again.

Saturday night made up for the tedium to some extent. Michael had declared it to be "cult cinema night", with midnight screenings of films for a devoted and, in some cases, debauched fan base. *The Sound Of Music* was especially popular, with the audience singing along to the soundtrack dressed as nuns, Nazis and Julie Andrews. Most fun of all were *Rocky Horror Picture Show* nights. The Splendide would be packed with punters in fancy dress who knew all the responses to shout at the screen and when to throw confetti, squirt water pistols and generally cause mayhem in the aisles. It seemed half the men in the area had been waiting for this excuse to dress up in drag, prancing around in basques, stockings and tiny knickers that often struggled to contain their cocks.

Michael, who sat in one of these shows, was surprised at just how enjoyably raucous proceedings became. When someone dressed as an usherette came on stage to perform a seductive burlesque routine to the film's opening song, a light bulb must have gone off over his head. On the following Monday, he called all the girls who worked as usherettes to a meeting so he could share his idea with us. He thought it would add to the spirit of proceedings if we made a special modification to our uniform on *Rocky Horror* nights. Specifically, he wanted us to leave our skirts off. I expected at least one of the girls to object, but no one did. Perhaps the others knew, just as I did, how downright horny we would look in our tight jackets and little hats with our stocking tops and suspenders blatantly on display. We fitted in perfectly with the kinky mood of the film, and sold so many snacks every time we appeared in our underwear Michael – only half-jokingly, I thought – suggested we dress like that all the time.

Much as I enjoyed the cult classic nights, I knew I was going to have to find some way of keeping the boredom at bay on quiet afternoons at the Splendide. The germ of an idea was planted one Wednesday or Thursday when I was helping a man to his seat after the screening had begun. I passed the love seats, which Michael was promoting as a special feature of the cinema, with "champagne packages" that offered bottles of fizz for couples to enjoy as they watched the film. In the circle of light from my torch, I caught the briefest glimpse of a man's hand cupping his lover's bare breast as they kissed, oblivious to what was happening on the screen. It didn't surprise me that couples grew amorous in the Splendide – the decadent surroundings and seats made for two practically demanded it – but that glimpse of naked female flesh was so unexpected, so deliciously rude, it had my juices flowing. Much as I wanted to linger to see whether things would progress further, the door at the back of the auditorium had opened and another patron was looking for his seat. With a small sigh of disappointment, I went to assist him. By the time I managed to sneak back to the love seats to get another look at the couple in action, she was buttoned up demurely once more and their attention was fully on the film.

My voyeuristic curiosity had been piqued, and I started making regular circuits of the auditorium during screenings, to see whether I could spot more naughty goings-on. In the dim light from the emergency exit signs I spotted plenty to fuel my erotic yearnings. It wasn't just lusty, deep-throated kissing and groping through clothes, though I saw plenty of that. Girls would have unzipped their boyfriend's fly and were slowly stroking his cock, or the lad would have his hand up her skirt as he fingered her. On one memorable occasion, a couple had manoeuvred themselves in one of the love seats so she was sitting on his lap. They appeared to be wrapped up in the fluffy romantic comedy they were watching, but I could tell from the gentle way she was rocking back and forth that she was impaled on his cock and fucking him to a slow climax. The sight was enough to have me slipping out of the room, knowing there was a good 25 minutes before Jennifer Aniston finally realised she'd been in love with her best friend since the start of the film and the credits started rolling. I dashed into the ladies' and locked myself in a cubicle. Hitching up my uniform skirt and pulling down my knickers, I rubbed my clit frantically 'til I came.

I would have gone on like that for ever, getting the odd guilty thrill to ease me through the day, if Michael hadn't scheduled the screening of a highly controversial French film. Billed as the story of a doomed love affair, it was actually little more than a series of highly graphic sex scenes. These, the publicity claimed, were not simulated.

Predictably, it attracted people who wouldn't normally sit through a foreign language film but simply wanted to watch the lead actor and actress fucking. Watching it for the first time, I couldn't decide whether the sex was real or staged, but it was certainly getting me horny. It seemed to be having the same effect on the audience. Normally, the soundtrack of any film the Splendide showed would be punctuated with the sound of sweets being unwrapped, coughing, even the odd phone ringing, despite the on-screen request that all mobiles had to be switched off. Today, there were no extraneous noises, just a tense, excited silence.

Almost without being aware of what I was doing, I unbuttoned my uniform jacket halfway down. I tweaked my nipple through my bra, feeling the little bud stiffen immediately. My pussy, hot and liquid, demanded my attention, and I would have stuck a hand up my skirt to satisfy the itch if I hadn't heard a sudden noise.

I tried to place the strangely familiar, rhythmic slapping sound. When I glanced round to see where it was coming from, I spotted a man sitting in the front row, a couple of feet from where I was standing. He had his cock in his hand and was wanking steadily. My mouth watered as I registered just how big it was. More than anything, I wanted to touch and taste it.

On feet that seemed to belong to someone else, I shuffled over to him. 'May I help you with that, sir?'

'What did you have in mind?' he asked.

There were empty seats to either side of him, and I dropped into one of them. I closed my fingers around his shaft. 'I figured you could use a hand with this,' I murmured. 'I saw how the film was turning you on.'

'Oh, it wasn't,' he said. 'I just have a thing about cute

redheaded usherettes. Watching you with your uniform half-undone, playing with your tits, was hornier than anything in this pretentious, self-regarding movie.'

My hand shuttled up and down his cock. 'So, you like me in this uniform, do you?'

'Mmm,' he replied, 'but I'd like it even more if you lost the skirt. Just like you do on *Rocky Horror* nights.'

So he was a regular here. Was he one of the men who squeezed into women's underwear to watch the film, unashamedly pervy and in touch with his feminine side, or was he a straitlaced Brad, needing to be introduced to the joys of filthy sex? So many delicious possibilities ...

I glanced to my left, then my right. No one was paying us the slightest attention. As the couple on screen were currently having vigorous sex on a kitchen table, that was hardly surprising. 'Since you ask so nicely ...' I reached behind me and unzipped my skirt. Then I stood briefly, so I could shimmy out of it, marvelling again at how much sexier it felt to where half a uniform, rather than a full one.

'And the knickers,' he said. 'Beautiful as they are, I need to see you without them.'

He was asking me to do something incredibly risky, but given he was already sitting with his cock out in the open I could hardly refuse. Not that I wanted to.

Knickerless, I dropped to my knees on the scratchy carpet and reached for his cock again. This time, I made an O of my red-painted lips and engulfed his helmet. He hissed through his teeth in pleasure as I swallowed more and more of him down. I was glad my pillbox hat was pinned securely in place, otherwise it would surely have fallen from my head as it bobbed vigorously in his lap. He must have been eating popcorn earlier, because I could taste the lingering traces of butter and salt he'd transferred from his palm as he wanked. It made me want to suck him until he came, but he whispered, 'Let me fuck you, pretty usherette.'

Obediently, I stopped what I was doing and climbed on to his lap, sitting so we were both facing the screen. I didn't believe I really needed the extra stimulation of watching the fictional couple have sex, but over the last few weeks I had come to the conclusion I was a born voyeur. With the subtitles conveying every last syllable of their dirty talk, I realised my lover was getting something out of the film, too, despite his earlier criticism. As the words 'Let me stick it up your arse' appeared in bold white type, I heard him give a lustful groan. That groan increased in volume as I slowly sank down on his cock, my pussy taking him in its tight, silken grip.

I bounced on his groin, loving the way his thick shaft filled me so exquisitely. He fumbled with the rest of my jacket buttons, undoing the garment completely. He kneaded my tits through my bra, his lips nuzzling my neck.

'God, that feels amazing,' I muttered. My hand dropped between my thighs, so I could roll my clit in small, tight circles. My vision was beginning to swim, the subtitles becoming a blur as my pleasure mounted. The dialogue on screen gave way to throaty grunts of uninhibited pleasure, echoing the noises we were making.

Beneath me, my lover's body stiffened and he came, clutching hard at my tits as he did. Throwing my head back, I let my own orgasm consume me, burning through me like a flash fire and leaving me spent.

When I finally mustered the strength to slip off his lap, I murmured, 'That was so good, but I'd better get dressed. I don't want to be caught like this when the lights go up.'

'Think what amazing publicity it would be for the Splendide,' he replied. 'Come along and see the film that's so horny it makes the usherettes fuck total strangers.'

'But you're not going to be a stranger, are you?' I asked as I scrambled back into my skirt, aware that we hadn't even exchanged names. 'I am going to see you again, aren't I?'

'Of course.' His tone was seductive. 'Saturday night is *Rocky Horror* night, and I'll be here.'

'How will I recognise you?' I asked, thinking of all the weird and wonderful costumes the audience chose to wear.

'Oh, I'll be easy to spot.' His next words gave me the feeling my life was about to become very interesting. 'I'll be dressed as an usherette.'

Cardboard
by Kay Jaybee

When Owen had asked Pia about her darkest, dirtiest dreams, her attention had most definitely been focused elsewhere. With his thick dick steadily pumping her snatch, and his agile fingers playing with her nipples, her concentration had been impaired. Consequently, when she'd confessed her most secret submissive desires, she hadn't been sure if Owen had actually heard her say that the smell of packaging that hung around him was as intoxicating to her as any drug. Or if he'd taken in the list of increasingly kinky things she'd like to happen to her amid a large pile of cardboard boxes.

After Pia had climaxed, she'd returned the question to him, but Owen's answer had been muffled by the soft skin he was kissing below her chest; Pia had been too consumed with renewed desire to hear the details of her lover's secret fantasies.

Waiting outside the courier depot, Pia watched the last two vans come in from their rounds, the drivers eagerly leaping from their vehicles and heading to reception. Automatically a blush started to spread across her cheeks as she wondered if they were as infused with the same mildly musty cardboard odour as Owen. Shaking herself to distract the erotic tableau that had appeared in her head, Pia fidgeted her feet against the pavement.

Where the hell had Owen got to? She could see his van, so he was definitely back from his round. Flicking a stray red hair up and under her green velvet cap, Pia checked her wristwatch. It was 6.45 p.m.; he was 20 minutes late. Heaving herself away from the wall against which she'd been propped, Pia walked towards the depot.

'Can I help?' An austere-looking woman behind the reception desk was buttoning up her overcoat,

Pia smiled politely, 'I'm waiting for Owen Richards.'

'Ah yes, he said he was expecting someone. He's in the staff room I think.' Then, with a swift point of her finger towards the dirty double doors to Pia's left, the woman disappeared into the grey evening.

Taking off her hat, and shaking out her wavy red hair, Pia hesitated. She'd never been inside the depot before, but as Owen had obviously left a message for her, she supposed it was all right to be there.

Pia gingerly eased open one half of the double doors. The tang of cardboard, paper and dust hit her senses with a wallop, causing her body to instantly react. The whole place smelt as delicious as Owen did after a day in the van. It was as if the scent of the materials he worked with day after day had become ingrained in the pores of his skin. Telling herself that soon she and Owen would be home, and she could work off the lust that was tingling through her veins, Pia walked into the staff room

The silence was vaguely eerie. Battered armchairs edged the room, and an overloaded coffee table was strewn with back copies of lads' magazines and unwashed coffee mugs. Yet there wasn't a driver in sight.

Deciding to return to the reception, Pia's hand was on the front door when she became aware of a presence behind her. She swung around and drew a sigh of relief when she saw Owen, 'Hell, you gave me a fright!'

'Sorry, babe.'

'Where've you been?'

'I had a few things to sort out. My mobile had no signal, so I left a message for you; I take it you got it?'

'The receptionist told me to wait in the staff room, but there was no one about so ...'

'... you thought you'd run away?'

Despite his twinkling brown eyes and lopsided smile, there was something about the tone of his voice that made Pia uneasy.

'Not run away exactly, but I didn't want to hang around in there on my own.'

Owen took hold of Pia's hand, 'We're rather shorthanded at the moment, so I have a few more things to do.' He ran a hand through her hair. 'Why don't you come with me?'

Pia allowed him to lead her back through the double doors, through the still empty staff room and on into the storeroom. The moment the door opened Pia drew in a sharp breath.

'Well?' Owen appeared unsure, and yet his eyes gleamed as he gripped his lover's hand tighter.

The store was cool, square and dimly lit, and even the dusty air seemed to have its own residual echo. Easing her hand from Owen's, Pia surveyed the deserted room.

The walls had rows of flat-packed cardboard boxes lined up all around them. Piles of plastic bags emblazoned with the company logo sat stacked in one corner, and three industrial-sized dispensers of parcel tape lay abandoned next to them. On the floor, a heavy layer of grime clung possessively to the surface, except for where someone had laid out a rectangle of squashed-down boxes, more or less in the size and shape of a king-sized bed.

Swallowing some moisture back into her throat Pia whispered, 'Is this what you've been sorting out?'

His reply of 'Yes' was barely audible as he waited for her reaction.

'So where is everybody?'

'It's Saturday evening, babe. Next shift doesn't start until six tomorrow.'

Even though the room was cold, Pia felt hot and uncomfortable in her coat and scarf. Unable to drag her gaze from the bed of cardboard, she said, 'I didn't think you'd heard me when I told you. You never said anything about my fantasy afterwards.'

'I heard most of it.'

As Owen's hands reached around her and started to undo the buttons of Pia's coat, her mind surged; *how much had he heard?*

Pia's eyes moved to the doors, 'But we can't! The door is unlocked, anyone could walk in.'

Owen produced a bunch of keys from his pocket, 'I'll lock the main door.'

Pia's pulse rate tweaked up a notch. *Could they really do this?* The smell of cardboard and the closeness of Owen, not to mention the wrongness of even being there, sent quivers of erotic excitement through her body. No one had ever tried to act out a fantasy for her before, not even half a fantasy.

'I'll go and lock the door then, shall I?'

Not trusting herself to speak, Pia just inclined her head.

Owen kissed her, his stubble scratching her face, his hands squeezing her shoulders through her coat. 'I won't be long.' His voice was husky, 'Lose the coat and wait for me on the cardboard.'

Watching him disappear through the door, Pia felt her palms grow clammy. Doubts were queuing up at the back of her head. *What if Owen doesn't lock the door properly? How can he be absolutely sure that there's no one left in this massive building? Do I even want to do this in real life – after all, shouldn't fantasies remain just that?*

'Why's your coat still on?' Owen's voice was accusing rather than amused.

'You were quicker than I expected.'

'Of course I was!' He wrenched the jacket from her shoulders, 'I'm about to see a beautiful woman writhe before me on a pile of cardboard.'

Pia's cheeks coloured violently, his brusque manner was in keeping with her dream, but totally foreign to his usual considerate nature. Owen unwound her scarf as she asked, 'Are you sure that it's OK? I don't want you getting the sack or anything.'

'I think you should leave the worrying to me. I also think you've said enough for the moment.' Bundling up Pia's hair, Owen scrunched it into a ponytail, which he tied with a collection of elastic bands he had wrapped around his wrist.

Her head spinning as Owen tugged her hair through the rubber loops, catching stray wisps painfully between his fingers, Pia shut her eyes, and inhaled slowly. The aroma of packaging filled her nostrils. She could almost taste it at the back of her throat. When she opened her eyes again, she found herself face to face with Owen. His expression killed any inclination she'd had to speak. A determination permeated with lust radiated from him, and Pia felt her tits swell beneath his stare.

'Strip.'

It was not an order that could be ignored. Pia's shaking hands began to fumble at her shirt buttons, her eyes glued to the bulge beneath Owen's black combats.

Shivering with a combination of cold and fear, standing in only her cream knickers and bra, Pia paused, goose-pimples breaking out across her skin.

'That'll do for now.' Owen's dark eyes shone at her, 'Now stand right in the middle of the boxes.'

Wordlessly she moved, her naked feet sinking against the uneven make-shift carpet, her toes shuffling away from the occasional rough corner. Fully aware of how turned on she was despite her misgivings, Pia could feel her silk panties sticking to her pussy.

Dragging his eyes away from his girl, Owen walked purposefully to the stack of plastic bags, and picked up one of the tape dispensers. Then, yanking Pia's arms behind her back, he caught her wrists in one hand, and deftly wrapped some tape around them.

'Owen, I ...'

He interrupted his lover before she could go on, 'You wanted to be dominated on a pile of cardboard boxes. It's too late to complain now it's happening.'

Pia opened her mouth to argue, but Owen's calloused hand came up quickly, and was pushed over her dry lips. 'If you can't keep quiet then I'll have to force you to.'

Surprised at how easily Owen had taken to this new role, Pia clamped her mouth together beneath his hand.

'That's better. Now sit down.'

Uncertainty flew through her as she sat cross-legged on the cardboard, curiosity at what might happen next arousing her still further. She kept telling herself that there was nothing to be afraid of, that Owen would never hurt her, but Pia couldn't help feeling a frisson of fear as hormones zipped through her body in passion-fuelled confusion.

Crouching before her, Owen smiled and, reverting to normal, said, 'You look incredible. How do you feel?'

'Good – I think.'

'Close your eyes.'

The second they were shut, the heady perfume of card and tape intensified the sensation of Owen's hands on her breasts. Pia was unable to contain a sigh of relief as he unfastened her bra, but when Owen pinched each teat, her sighs became voluble squeals.

'I told you to be quiet. I'll have to silence you.'

Pia's eyes shot back open, 'But ...'

Owen was shaking his head as though he was bitterly disappointed. 'You've proven you can't be trusted.' He picked the parcel tape back up.

Before Pia could protest, Owen sealed her mouth with a neat rectangle of beige tape. As the sticky surface adhered to her lips, Pia tried to stop her chest pounding with panic. Adjusting to breathing to just through her nose; she looked and felt like a kidnap victim.

Owen nodded in satisfaction, 'Beautiful.'

As tears of shock gathered at the corners of Pia's eyes, he added, 'Beautiful, powerless, and silent.'

Throwing the tape to one side, Owen's hands began to fondle the soft flesh of her chest, while licking the moisture away from her eyes.

Pia's body readily responded to his touch and, as Owen's fingers dropped into her lap, teasing her stomach, prickles of longing shot up and down her spine. Staring into her eyes, Owen took his hands lower still, making Pia's breath shallower as he danced his fingertips around the edge of her knickers. Then, holding her gaze, he cupped her mound firmly in one hand.

'You hot hussy,' He stroked a stray hair from over her eyes, 'a helpless hussy. So gorgeous.'

Pia wished she could speak, wished she could reach out and caress his body, handle the muscles in his arms, scratch her nails across his flesh, but she had no choice but to sit, the edges of the boxes digging into her backside.

'In fact,' Owen tilted his head in mock contemplation, 'I think it's a real shame there's no one else here to see how fantastic you look.'

Pia's heart skipped a beat. Suddenly she knew how wrong she'd got things. He hadn't only heard part of her mumbled fantasy, he'd heard it all. She'd been the one who hadn't been paying enough attention when they'd discussed their deepest desires, not him.

Owen stroked Pia's cheek with one hand, and kneaded her pussy with the other, staining the fabric of her panties with her juices, 'I couldn't believe my luck when you told me your submissive dream. To be shagged by two men at the same time on cardboard. You really are my dirty little girl, aren't you?'

Pia frantically shook her head, the reality of other men seeing her vulnerable body hitting her in a wave of nervous adrenaline.

'Oh no, baby,' Owen gripped her crotch tighter, using it to lever her to a standing position. 'I don't believe you really want to leave. I think this is what you want; your body certainly agrees with me.' He reinforced his claim by jabbing a hand inside her knickers, making Pia inwardly groan with pleasure. Bringing his fingers straight back out again, he showed his lover the glistening liquid that stuck to his skin. Licking Pia's juices away, he said, 'You couldn't want this more if you tried, and as you would know if you'd been listening, I'd just love to watch your dream in action.'

As if Owen's words had been a pre-planned cue, the door to the storeroom opened, and the two drivers Pia had seen earlier walked in.

Pia's pulse pounded manically as Owen greeted his guests. 'This is Pia, Pia this is Andy and Craig. I think they'll fit your requirements.'

Stunned, Pia just stood there, conscious of nothing but the new arrivals' eyes as they mentally removed her underwear. They were so near to her that she could smell the same incredible aroma of sweat and cardboard that Owen shared, and the uncertainty that had knotted in her gut was swamped by a hot flush of erotic anticipation. Dressed in the same uniform of green polo-shirt and black combats, all three men oozed an air of barely tamed lust.

Andy, tall and slim, his blond hair short and spiked, stood to her right. The stockier figure of Craig, his head shaved, his eyes as emerald as his shirt, waited, poised, to her left.

Pia's legs began to shake as Owen bent his lips to her ear, 'They are so hot for you. So fucking hot, and I'm gonna watch them have you.'

Her shoulders quivered as his breath tickled her skin and, with eyes that pleaded for reassurance, she peered up at him.

Slipping back into his usual calm voice, Owen muttered so that only she could hear, 'Don't worry, you'll love it. I promise,' before stepping back and roughly pulling off her sodden underwear.

Placing a hand on each of his colleague's shoulders, Owen steered them to the far corner of the room, leaving Pia to imagine what they were saying to each other.

After what seemed to have been a lifetime, the couriers strode purposefully back towards her, their faces creased with hunger and disbelief, as if neither of them could believe their luck. Standing at the edge of the cardboard, directly in front of Pia, the three men tore off their shirts. Pia's muffled gasp of appreciation turned to frustration at not being able to hold either her lover's chest, or the other toned torsos.

Abruptly, in one simultaneous move, Andy and Craig attached their mouths to Pia's breasts. The contrasting texture and pressure from each set of lips, kissing, licking and biting her, felt incredible. Shutting her eyes once more, Pia was grateful for the warm hands that not only snaked over her body, but also supported it, as her limbs shook against the cardboard.

Their digits were everywhere at once, between her legs, over her clit, behind her knees, on her neck, as though each man was on his own personal race against time to get as much out of the encounter as possible before Owen changed his mind about them fucking his girlfriend.

Her head swimming, bright colours exploded behind Pia's eyelids. All fear forgotten, her whole body began to tighten with a climax that coursed through her so quickly she thought she'd collapse.

Seeing her legs begin to buckle, Owen stepped forward and lowered Pia to the ground, ripping off her gag. Pia cried out as the tape plaster tore mercilessly at her skin, but the new vision before her more than made up for the moment's discomfort.

Andy and Craig had removed the rest of their clothes, and stood, towering over her naked body. The cardboard bed crackled beneath their combined weight and, with her hands still trapped uncomfortably behind her back, Pia braced herself.

The drivers glanced at each other, as if to confirm some previously discussed plan of action, before falling to their knees either side of her.

A pair of calloused hands flipped her onto her stomach, so that her head was buried in the boxes, and the overpowering scent of the card shot straight into Pia's nostrils, making her expel a protracted moan of need. Her previous orgasm was already forgotten, all that mattered was the next one.

Two hands grasped her buttocks, and two others pushed her legs up and out at the knees, so all her weight was centred on her face and shoulders as they dug into the rough bed. A pair of bare legs appeared before her. Owen had stripped.

Pia's blood pounded in her cricked neck as she felt a single finger begin to rub at her clit. She didn't care who the finger belonged to, just that it kept moving, as she mewled into the packaging.

Then her hands were picked up at the wrists, and one of the couriers plucked away the tape that bound Pia's wrists. She couldn't help but scream, as the sticky surface ripped minute hairs from her skin.

Without giving her time to adjust to her freedom, Pia was ordered to her hands and knees. A hand seized her ponytail and wrenched her neck high. Pia blinked at Craig's thickly erect dick, which hovered just out of reach. She longed to take it between her teeth; the thought of Owen watching her; of him wanting her to do this, making Pia hornier than ever.

With his cock in his hand, Craig began to play it around Pia's parted mouth. At the same time, she heard a condom packet being opened, and Andy came up behind her, grabbing her left hip with one hand, he began to tease his dick over and around her wet snatch with the other.

This was agony. Pia was desperate to engulf the shaft before her, but that would mean shifting fractionally forward and losing the touch of the cock brushing her from behind. At the same time, she urgently wanted to be full of the rod teasing her pussy, but didn't want to shift backwards and lose the fragile contact of the cock at her lips.

Pia could see Owen, a broad grin across his face, a palm wrapped around his penis as he slowly caressed it back and forth. Unconsciously, Pia began to rock against the cardboard in time to her lover's masturbation, so one second she was close to the cock at her mouth, the next, grazing against the one at her snatch.

With each movement, the need Pia felt to keep going increased, and she began to speed up, working herself off against the two men, who somehow managed to keep still as her tongue flicked over the tip of one, and her clit bumped the head of the other.

Her breasts swinging manically beneath her, there was no way Pia could stop now. With closed eyes, she was immersed in a world where only sensation mattered, where only the briefest touch of the two men, the smell of cardboard, and the sound of Owen's heavy breathing mattered.

Perspiration began to gather on her forehead and between her breasts. Suddenly it was too much, and Pia let out a strangled cry of frustration. She needed to be full. She needed two cocks inside her, and she needed them now.

Breaking the rhythm, she lunged forward and caught Craig's length between her teeth. Terrified he'd back away, Pia held him firmly in her throat. He didn't move however, but called out to Owen, 'Fuck she's good.' While Andy shuffled forward, impaling her cunt in one swift move.

Pia's climax immediately hammered through her. Thrusting and pumping their friend's girl, both men were so consumed with the need to come themselves, they didn't seem to notice when Pia shuddered, her body jacking with pleasure. Pinioned between the drivers, her muscles slackened, and she only managed to remain on all fours, due to the pressure of their hard bodies, as each raced the other to spunk inside her first.

Her mouth filled with salty liquid, only seconds before Andy's dick exploded inside her snatch. Gulping frantically, Pia wasn't able to catch it all, and her chin dripped with seed as Craig pulled away from her face.

The moment the men were spent, they backed off, and Pia crashed to the squashed bed, panting hard.

Owen, his shaft still stiff in his hand, rolled Pia onto her back, and showered her chest with a warm rain of come. Then he turned to his colleagues and, with a nod of dismissal, they gathered their clothes and left.

Kneeling, Owen gently wiped the sweat from Pia's face, and cradled her in his arms, 'You OK?'

Smiling up at him, she nodded.

'You were amazing. Totally incredible.'

Her throat too dry to speak, Pia placed her head on his lap, and took a long deep breath, enjoying one final lungful of the scent of the cardboard bed, now improved by the lingering aroma of a fantastic double fuck.

COCKTALES

VOLUME ONE

When a girl who loves men in uniform meets a hunky fireman, they're soon heating up the station …

Showing herself off to her boyfriend's flatmate is the start of her webcam career …

A trip into the New Zealand countryside introduces a city girl to the delights of bareback riding…

Lust, desire and sex from the best names in erotic fiction, including Justine Elyot, K D Grace and Sommer Marsden

COCKTALES

VOLUME TWO

In the secluded clearing, she puts on the show of a lifetime for a sexy stranger ...

Cyber sex distracts her from her dull office job, but who's she really talking dirty to ...?

Swapping partners shows a neglected girlfriend all the delights she's been missing ...

These are just some of the explicit encounters from the best names in erotic fiction, including Charlotte Stein, Jade Taylor and Sommer Marsden

Join us on Facebook

www.facebook.com/xcite.erotica
www.facebook.com/XciteGay
www.facebook.com/XciteBDSM

Follow us on Twitter

@XciteBooks
@XciteGay
@XciteSpanking

www.xcitebooks.com

Scan the QR code to join our mailing list